Southword 48

Southword is published
by Southword Editions
an imprint of the
Munster Literature Centre
Frank O'Connor House
84 Douglas Street
Cork City T12 X802
Ireland

www.munsterlit.ie

/munsterlitcentre.bsky.social

/southwordjournal

/munsterliteraturecentre

#Southword

Issue 48
ISBN 978-1-915573-17-9

Editor
Patrick Cotter

Seán Ó Faoláin International Short Story Competition Judge
Camilla Grudova

Gregory O'Donoghue International Poetry Competition Judge
Mary O'Malley

Southword Subscribers' Competitions Judge
James O'Leary

Production
James O'Leary

Thank you to Anne Kennedy for her technical assistance

Cover Image: *The Rook's Funeral* by Fidelma Massey

The Munster Literature Centre is a grateful recipient of funding from

CONTENTS

Poems **57**

Kosoluchi Agboanike
Dean Browne
Eithne Carson
Pratibha Castle
Eithne Cavanagh
Polina Cosgrave
John F. Deane
Ajla Dizdarević
John FitzGerald
Nicola Geddes
Jake M.M. Griffin
Emilie Jelinek
Kasimma
Emily Anna King 锡萍芳
Kapu Lewis
Aoife Lyall
Simon Maddrell
Lorraine McArdle
Sinéad McClure
David McLoghlin
Jenny Mitchell
Jennifer Nevergole
Mary O'Donnell
Brian Obiri-Asare
Jane Satterfield
Colm Scully
Dechen Shaw
Stephen Spratt
Paul Sutherland
Molly Twomey
Julijana Velichkovska
Stuart Watson

Please Subscribe

By subscribing, you will receive new issues of *Southword* straight from the printers, as quickly as we will ourselves. Your subscription will also help to provide us with the resources to make *Southword* even better.

Other perks include access to *Southword Online*, the precursor to the print journal as you know it now. These 27 issues, which appeared on our website from 2009 – 2018, include ten years of writing from our O'Donoghue poetry competition and Ó Faoláin short story competition. You will also have the opportunity to enter our free-to-enter flash fiction competition and poetry competition exclusively for subscribers. Current subscribers are emailed a link every April and may submit up to three poems and/or three pieces of flash fiction; winners are published in our summer issue and receive the following: 1st Prize €150, 2nd prize €100, 3rd prize €75.

Rates for two issues per year:

Ireland, UK, North America, Australia, New Zealand	€24 *postage free*
Rest of Europe	€28 *postage free, tax-inclusive*
Rest of the World	€34 *postage included*

For subscriptions and renewals visit munsterlit.ie.

Southword may also be purchased issue-by-issue through Amazon outlets worldwide and select independent booksellers.

Southword Editor's Poetry Award
Lucy Holme

I Used to Weave Stories

—after Sappho

I was once in violation, delinquent in the belly
of a subway, waiting for a signal, stranded in a skein
of alleyways, in what was once known as *la superba:*

a nickname that also suited him well. I used to walk
the narrow lanes, buildings warped as Aleppo pines.
I used to knife's edge, to clock watch, beleaguered points

until they'd rust, used the thrill of our illegality to steel
my nerves. Coveted language, was buoyed by false cognates.
Like a rogue wire, I threatened to trip: feet, hearts, switches—

tethered myself to a translated version of romance,
I fed coins into the slot to light electric candles,
bowed in the shadows to deceased saints.

I used to read novels about the true meaning of luxury—
they made me profligate with attention.
I could not retain a single word of advice.

Unreasonably attached to peril, I used to wonder
who would wait a lifetime to be used like that,
then pronounce it the deepest love they have ever known:

only somebody starving, but still hopeful, I used to think.
I pitied people like me. Those in thrall to the young and vital,
pulled from one life to another, a patchwork of intent

and chance, neither understood nor truly desired,
but compelled to discover. I was tangled in our addictive
malinteso, cut out patterns, like local rissëu. Followed the mosaic

through Molo Vecchio to Via Roma, past the fountain.
Used to stall and change the subject, embroider facts
and pretend that he loved me more than I loved him.

I used to hide under churchyard cloisters—scaled the convent
walls to glean historical folly, spilled a trail of lies,
like breadcrumbs, used to—

finish what I had started—

and was once a navigator, braided a coarse rope
and hammered it to the city walls to map his route to me,
but would always go to him. Always ready for his text,

awake long after he had gone. Chewing my nails
until the ragged edges bled. I used to be unrecognisable,
and late at night, in dive bars and churches alike

I held tight to the hand of my fictional adversary,
following him to the port, down to the breakwater,
trying to work him out, like a fishbone caught in my braces.

Anatoli 1989

—after Helen Chadwick

I follow a coastal road to an island town. There, we crack pink crab legs,
squeeze lemon from a little muslin bag tied with a bow. Piling the shells,
we shuck the grey gnarled overcoats from oysters, flint and shallot brine
shrivelled, swallow them whole with greedy abandon. You refuse the mussels,
their orange bellies and billy-goat beards always made you feel sick
and below a full moon of slick foam, I note how the lids snap shut
when my fork comes near. Under a silver cloche hides a pigeon wing,
flesh barely seared, garnished only with your sardonic replies. We were
fashioned from hot oil, re-modelled like fresh loukoumades. Broken into pieces,
licked from each other's fingers. Fast forward to Anatoli—and I am eight
drafts in again on a brand new poem that leaves out everything true.
I watch a reel of Paris Starn snipping off the end of a freshly baked doughnut
with a pair of kitchen scissors and am suddenly crying as she pipes in Chantilly
cream and framboise, thinking of forgotten dates, of unfillable holes.

Molecular Gastronomy

—after Lyn Hejinian

I.M. ML

The other day I searched online for the story and a photo of you
popped up, carrying a bag, heading some place exotic with your list.
It made no sense—three of you gone in the same year. Young men,
two sandy-haired and one darker, older. Like you were all vying

for most unbelievable death. I think you won. In the beginning,
I imagine it felt just like flying. I had never been to the Far East,
but I knew what it was to be drunk and high in the back of a taxi
at 30, alive with new ventures, bathed in a symphony of light.

Full tilt, danger out of frame, two buses and a hill that has grown,
over the years, to San Franciscan proportions; the precipitousness,
the pitch, the terror, the sirens. Back home, at the local supermarket
they gathered to buy the simplest food possible for a chef's wake,

while you lay alone in a mortuary. A stuffy pub backroom filled up
with well-meaning relatives bearing baskets of high-end deli products
and obscure ingredients—truffle oil, white miso, Pitcairn honey,
gorgonzola just the right side of putrid, jars of neon peperoncinos.

The intentions were good; to save her if they couldn't save you
(everyone has to eat to live) but all this just made things worse
because you would never cook again. You were the *Swedish National.*
The papers hadn't named you yet. What would it be like without you?

There was no life without haute cuisine. Something transcendent
conjured from the most inauspicious of groceries. A recipe for charcoal,
ashes and a 64° egg, cut out and stuck to the fridge. Their memories
could remain perfectly spherical, unimpeded by horror crash headlines.

It was art but could it ever be a comfort? Food became ever plainer
until it was no longer distinguishable from air. Maybe you were there
in that English village fused at its core with Scandinavian hospitality.
Your poor mother, who could ever forget seeing her so distraught?

But even if your body was absent that day, you were the hazy morning
fog rolling in from the Thames, and like the oak-smoked Saint-Pierre
you presented to our guests table-side in Ajaccio, the summer before,
it just took time for us to understand what it was. I didn't dream of you

until two weeks later; there you were in soft-focus, wiping down fridges,
shoulders stooped, crouching over your clogs. And I am back in that year
of wasted potential, brakes off, spinning, trying to recall each experiment,
how it tasted, smelled, what impressions remained after the smoke cleared.

Dancing with Thierry Thieû Niang

Lani O'Hanlon

When he comes to dance in the hospital,
Blanche is ninety-years old, back straight and hollow
as bamboo, a scarf of blue roses around her throat.

His cheekbones and brown eyes call up memories
of warriors and his father's ancestors from Vietnam.
He dances around the day room on muscular, springy legs

but she sees the first greys in his shiny straight hair
when she takes his hand to read his palm.
He asks her to dance. She tries: still holding a stick

in her right hand, left hand clutching his arm.
Her slippered feet stutter along. Other residents
and staff watch, attentive as swallows on a wire.

Thierry leads a waltz, his cushiony cheek
against her moth thin skin. There is music –
a woman singing in French. Thierry cradles Blanche

in his arms and begins to spin, slow at first then rapidly.
She lies back entranced, one willowy arm
trails through currents of air. She smiles – a moon

in winter reflecting the far away sun.
Thierry goes down on one knee like a knight.
She perches on his knee, their foreheads kiss.

Embodied in that day room – Shakti
and Shiva beyond thought – beyond age.
But the dance must end.

Thierry walks her back down
the institutional corridor to her room.
Her head bows towards her slippers.

'What's going on Blanche?'
A moment of hesitation then she whispers 'Je t'Aime.'

Note: After watching the French documentary *Une jeune fille de 90 ans (A young girl in her 90's)* with dancer and choreographer Thierry Thieû Niang who visits care homes and hospitals bringing dance to the residents.

ÉTUDE 149
Ray Malone

at every instant an elsewhere, a narrowing before a way
opens, wild surmise or a smile, or the sunlight through a leaf
for a second, attention's everything, to what's to be seen, what
heard, what felt as the shell fragments and the piece designed to
penetrate pierces the flesh, that other flesh, that foreignness,
to bury itself beneath it, beyond imagining, being blind to it:
the moment goes, a breast distracts, and the same petal fades,
the eye cast into yet another darkness, a further shade of forgetting,
a distant memory, and only seconds ago, so fiercely lit, so
full of a light, so open to the sight of it:
something falls from the wall, that hung there, the space
it occupied empty, who was there to witness it, to say
what it once meant, what its absence bodes, what omen of
good or ill, what man or woman might find a meaning for it,
a name for the strange place it made, where nothing reigns
but silence, and the mind's complicity:
elsewhere, that other place, where the rain of bombs lays
waste to words, somewhere in the gap between them,
thin as a leaf, strips them of meaning, beyond smiles
and the melting emptiness, where the sun
in a sudden flash sears through everything,
and the leaf itself disappears from sight

Note: 'Shell' used by the IDF with 'added fragmentation liner' designed to cause maximum injury (*Guardian* article 11 July 2024).

3rd Prize, Gregory O'Donoghue International Poetry Competition

Running Away

Clive McWilliam

He rushed in, full pelt.
I was brushing up split ends
and sun stood live behind him in the shop door—

come on pet let's go—
we were only two months in
but keen as they come—Paul

Shiny Paul who'd just climbed down from his crane
swaying through each day in the wind
dazzled by distance, the hint of hope

the odd load of bricks
to swing over the town
then coming down each night with the sun

combed and proud as an astronaut
to tell me what he'd dreamed today
between each load he'd shifted.

Shiny Paul taking my hand with a moisturised grip
and me in stilettos, still heady
with lacquer and airblown tales

emptying sinks as I pass,
hitching my tight skirt high
as we rush from the shop full pelt

breathless with everything that's ahead
we dash through town where boys on bikes
with no brakes try to follow

and locals knowing the day of all days has begun
wave from their windows where evening flashes
off and on in our faces like a film

and my hand slips in and out
of *Shiny Paul's* fingers
as we swarm up the sun coming down Bee Lane.

Tallyman

Anne Connolly

Oh Rabbie Burns you might have gone
to the sugar-land of plenty
and who's to say you'd not have been
a strutting man so kenty
making a bonny living there
upon the backs of slaves who stooped
and struggled with the weight
that bought them early graves?

The beauty of the red, red rose
must wither in the heat
the sweetness of the laverock's tune
must fade beneath the beat
of Africa in broken hearts
that could no longer take
the high road or the low road
as the dawn began to break.

Their only choice a skelping sun
or a tawse against the skin.
If you'd been there would you have cried their labour was a sin?
Would you have winched a tidy lass
who couldn't answer no
though dark defiance in her eyes
was proof that it was so?

Oh Rabbie, sad as it may be
that you died before your prime
"A man's a man for aw that"
and you said it for all time.

Song from the Lower Level

Kurt Luchs

When I was three we lived briefly
in a Chicago basement tenement
I can't recall the number or the street
only that it was summer
and hot even before dawn with the dirty
window cracked open to let in the breeze

except there was no breeze in the Windy City
rather a ceaseless parade of pedestrians
at street level above our heads
bits of voices snatches of conversations
women's high heels trying to keep up
with men's dress shoes as the whole town

rushed to work or sauntered back from it
we got them coming and going
their din woke us up and put us to sleep
with the late sun dripping on the window
like red rain even today I still
find myself judging people by their voices

and their shoes it may seem shallow
but it's not often wrong nor am I
surprised when their staccato words
hang unfinished in the summer air
like the city like civilization like life
or pigeon feathers drifting to the molten sidewalk

To map a leaf

Joanne McCarthy

(i)

Tim Robinson raises an ash leaf in Clare, asks us to *consider how big this leaf is to you, to me, how big it is to a cow or an ant, to consider the veins, and the scurry over veins to go from one end of the leaf to another, to consider how important one crack in the limestone of the Burren is to a family of ants.*

He leans over pages of folded landscapes, topographical references to path, cave and pothole, notes on a strange field, on when the last O'Donovan died in a house, on where a turlough appears and reappears, on where the tale of the hag begins. Our eyes trace his detailing of individual rocks, placing of precise contours; thousands of black marks on a stony grain.

(ii)

In Cork, I climb Donovan's Hill, scan Six-Inch maps in the college library, fields chain-surveyed before the Great Hunger, charted boundaries of river, bog, wood, and boulder. Uplands as blank open spaces. Contours of a landscape in mutation.

(iii)

Roughly two hundred years after the Six-Inch maps were drawn, I wonder about the guide who worked on the maps in my home townland, the unnamed local who selected what ring fort to point out, what story of the megalithic tomb to share.

How did the triangulation team chart their way through the bog at Portalocha? or up the hill to ArdCillín? Who showed them the path through the rocks? Did they mention the story about the dead horsewoman or did they keep that to themselves?

(iv)

Google Maps does not show Ardcillín. It shows Ardkilleen. No variation of Portalocha. If I drop a pin to where I know Portalocha exists, Google says I can walk to Ardkillen in forty-six minutes. Google knows nothing of the right of way through Josie Moore's, that walking up the Céim Road to Castletown and back around the main road is madness when you can go through the fields.

(v)

Josie is dead now and The Hollies Centre for Sustainability is on his land, the locals call them the hippies, and Dommo drained the lake and bog at Portalocha. He is quarrying stone too. I'm not sure the hippies honour the right of way anymore.

(vi)

My uncle owns land in Ardcillín. High burial place. An old casket was found in a sand pit there once, six feet long by two and a half feet wide, all cleaned out. A *gallán* standing stone near it was knocked down, it was one of six in a line separating O'Leary land from the Hughs. I could go up there amongst the dead and ask them if I can name them. Or consider them.

Playing with Bullet Holes in the Upholstery

Paul McMahon

No one knows when we are going to arrive,
the inspector said, pointing to the fog outside,
as I stood in the crowded aisle of a stalled train
somewhere between New Delhi and Varanasi
with visibility outside the window just extending
beyond the tracks where the shadows of trees
loomed like characters huddled in grey blankets

as the closing door of a compartment opened
another in my head when I was ten years old
in the passenger seat of our red Ford Cortina
playing with bullet holes in the upholstery
one foggy morning as my father drove me
to school on the Falls Road while teaching me
the lyrics to The Town I Loved So Well

and although I was yet to see The Ganges
I can say that it resembled the Falls Road
because I drifted down that river in a rowboat
the following dawn through thick river fog
as the stoned boatman rolled another spliff
and the ancient temples of Varanasi

lined the riverbank like The Rock Bar,
St. Dominic's Grammar, the derelict fountain
shrining Waterville Park, and accompanying
the processions to the cremation fires burning
in the Ghats on the riverside, the temple gongs
rang out like the bells of Clonard Cathedral

and like the bullet holes beside me in the car,
the small holes in the bottom of the boat
seeped water around my feet but didn't sink us –
and like the shrouded stone-weighted children
dropped from boats into The Ganges by fathers
whose journey to the river would never end

my terminally ill father gripping the wheel
drove on down The Falls, down The Ganges,
and I'm still in the aisle of that stalled train
somewhere between New Delhi and Varanasi
playing with bullet holes in the upholstery
listening to my father singing me the lyrics to
his favourite song, The Town I Loved So Well.

The Yellow Bell
Paul McMahon

In 2697 BC, Emperor Huang-di
sent his chief mathematician
and most gifted musician, Ling-Lun,

to the western mountains of China,
on the border with India,
where the finest bamboo grew, to cut

perfect eleven-month-old bamboo
pipes, so they could record the note
that had been blowing overhead

within a piercing sonic wind
for the previous three years
at the edge of the northern desert.

☆

The note blown by that wind,
said Huang-di, was the true tone
of the world. And to this pitch

Ling-Lun would cut his bamboo,
so that all other court instruments
could be tuned to it – and from the note

made by Ling-Lun's bamboo tubular bell,
all music would ascend in twelve steps
until reaching the next octave,

its double, its uncast shadow, the cloak
worn by all music when singing
the colour it is born with.

☆

So, on a Spring morning, in 2697 BC,
under a blessing of cherry blossom confetti,
Emperor Huang-di's chief mathematician

and most gifted musician, Ling-Lun,
set off alone towards the western mountains.
Twelve months later, when he returned

with his bamboo bells, the sonic wind was still
blowing at the edge of the northern desert,
and under the drone of that tempest

Ling-Lun cut The Yellow Bell, capturing
the original vibration for the note we call *Do*,
the fundamental tone of the world.

Donatello's Magdalene

Elisabeth Murawski

He dresses her in tangles
of her hair,

gives her deep-set eyes
like trees hollowed

out by fire
dark as the ocean floor,

the ninth hour.
And hands

with long thin fingers
not quite

touching, raised
before her,

holding nothing
but the air.

Not mad, focused
on the desert

in which
she finds herself

finding him:
a woman shockingly in love

and stripped
to the bone.

Another sonnet in praise of darkness

Jenny Pollak

It isn't hard to find a hundred reasons to be glad.
You, with your whole heart, and the sea simmering in the light.
It isn't hard, with the chant of cicadas,
as good a choir as you'll get on a weekend at the height of summer.
The trees on the headland are happy after the rain and lean forward.
The honey bees—what can be said of them that isn't a celebration—
whose work finishes in such sweetness you could be forgiven for thinking
you were already in paradise.

If the wind picks up too strongly, if the people seem at cross purposes
with the earth, the land subdued by a history so steeped in sadness
it only becomes itself the further away it gets from the houses. If blood materialises
in every sentence you start, and the sound of the ferry growls too deeply
to stay completely free of the darkness, you'll know you've been both burdened
and blessed with a vision you are honour bound to carry.

Hymns

Réré Ukponu

When the doors close the women in church sing
Kpo Ya Chukwu oga nu – call on God and he will hear.
In church the women are clay pots, deeply grooved and mango juice sticky.
The expansion of each breath pressing on the earth joints,
on the fault lines underneath the belly.
With every swallow the water sloshes against the lip.
The men stand at the door, with wide gaping mouths, with quarry cut
shoulders, with gravestone teeth and mildew breath.
Their necks leashed with ties.
The children smell like *omebe* soup. Scent leaf for sickness, *utazi* for pain
and pumpkin leaf for sweetness.
The bell rings and the service begins.
They all ignore the dead at the door.

Kpo Ya, Call on –
In the thicket of your hair, your mother gets to gardening.
Milk flower, freesias, poppies.
Those long fingered, baby bird knuckled hands, weave trinity braids –
like a skipping rope, like a thread, like a noose.
When she turns your head to the side, you feel the weight of her quiet like
a hot stone.
The air smells like lavender.

Chukwu, no – God will
You ask why she stayed; you press down on the tender spot on your wrist,
feel the bracket of her knees.
She doesn't answer – instead she says:
I kept all your scabs *Inneh,* the red burgundy paint chips, the molten lava
middle, I ate them whole.
The clean whistle laugh of you,
The bright brown nut butter bean smile of you.
The spice snap sizzling scent of you.
I gobbled them up.
When the man came home, I was so full I had no room for flinching.
The sky outside is the colour of a heart breaking.

The women in church close the door, sing
Kpo Ya Chuku no Gaza – call on God and he will answer.
You see your mother in the mirror, the same chin, and widespread eyes.
The punch of her lips.
The magpie swoop of her brow, inviting sorrow, its cry singular and afraid.
This is your answer.

Titian puts down his paintbrush and picks up his guitar

Roger West

mussel shell tuna fin cuttlefish ink
pyrite powder azurite zinc

cerulean celadon cadet and celeste
crows wing gull feather robin egg ravens nest

midnight diamond byzantine slate
imperial prussian palatinate

the heart of the spark at the heart of the flame
ferrocyanide blood in the vein

kingfisher starfish silver lake and capri
peacock periwinkle anemone

indigo aqua ultramarine
french fig and damson and aubergine

cornflour columbine lapis lazuli
indian ocean mediterranean sea

ice cap polar night magnetic ash
rock salt and cobalt thunderbolt flash

berber and breton ceylon and chartreuse
jesuit sacristan la vierge douleureuse

turquoise and teal tiffany true
woke up this morning, baby, I had all of those blues
yeah woke up this morning, baby, I had all of those blues

Snap
Jack Kennedy

1st Prize, Seán Ó Faoláin International Short Story Competition

Leon's howling in the en-suite. I'm on the sprawled bedsheets, springs digging into my back. Even in my knickers, I'm far too hot: the window only opens a smidge, and the night is warm and still. The yellowish street-light covers my bare skin.

Maybe I should bring him a glass of water. Pat his back. Coo at him softly.

Instead, I fiddle with my phone, and flick through our little photo album.

***

There we are in Dublin Airport. Smiling expectantly at the camera, the bags under our bloodshot eyes failing to trump our enthusiasm. As always, he's near perfect: hair styled in a very precise mess, just the right amount of bristly stubble hugging his jawline. An easy smile.

– Will ye hurry up to fuck, Caitríona?

Just out of shot, a mother rocked a screaming baby in her arms. The baby glared at me: his face a red mucosal knot.

– The noise, Leon…

– I hope to fuck he's not comin' with us.

We can be as nasty as we want together.

***

Next, Leon is holding up a pint of Guinness, winking at the camera. He's centred in the frame, the departures bar a soft blur behind him.

He slugged down the pint, while I sipped at my flat white. All around us rowdy holidaymakers drank and shouted away the early hours. Voices bounced off the tiles, metallic sounding and overwhelming. Dancing Queen barely audible underneath. It smelled of grease and egg and beer and unfamiliar sweat.

– Split the G.

He licked the cream off his upper lip and grinned at me. I couldn't help but smile back. Leon's joy has always been contagious.

***

Next: a shot of Leon sleeping on the budget airline blue. His head is back on the headrest, his mouth hanging open.

Before I took it, I wiped away the thin droplet of drool adhering to his mouth. He looked cute, sure, but I'd hardly go post a picture of him with a glob of spit hanging off his lips.

Here and now, I sort of wish I had not. It's missing something, maybe a little bit of saliva.

He was snoring softly, dead to the world. I tried to read, but the words refused to stick. I always envied him for his complete ease, wherever he is and whatever he's doing.

***

An obligatory picture of us in the hotel mirror. Me: a tiered, floral pink dress, tight on the waist but flowing down my legs. Soft chiffon, that swishes with each step. White trainers, to keep it comfy and casual. French tip nails. Mink lashes. Wavy hair, freshly blow-dried. My tan even and borderline believable, the few streaky bits hidden from view. Leon had done my back, and it turned out about as well as I had expected.

Leon: an untucked, artfully creased white shirt, black chinos and Docs. A stud glistens in his right ear. No effort, yet he still manages to look as if he has a team of stylists on-call.

***

Next, the two of us standing with our arms wrapped around each other, beneath the mediaeval bulk of the Belfry. Soft sunlight swaddles us.

– I'm fucken starving, Caitríona.

The old man smiled awkwardly at me as he passed back my phone.

– Dank je.

All around us were brasseries and cafés and day drinkers strung out on outdoor tables. Bruges. Like a medieval theme park until you noticed the Burger King sitting in a wonderfully ornate building. 'Home of the Flame-Grilled Whopper', the sign proclaimed.

***

Next: a precise, Wes Anderson type shot for dinner. For me: a steaming pot of mussels, with frites on the side, and a glass of strawberry kriek. On Leon's side, a hamburger and chips with a pint of lager.

– Can I eat now?

– Yeah, go on.

He grabbed the burger and bit into it with a greasy squelch, before washing it down with a slug of lager. I gingerly fiddled with my mussels, trying to use the empty shells to scoop out the innards of other shells. Hard work, but fun in a fidgety way. Leon slammed down his empty pint, and raised his hand for another.

– Thirsty?

– I'm on me holibops, babe.

He grinned that mind-melting smile, and I just smiled and sipped at my kriek. The square was half empty and hushed, the lovely amber streetlamps just starting to light up, the sky dissolving slowly into navy blue.

***

Dessert: a glass of cherry kriek and some pint of lager, with the square as a backdrop. Figures are in frozen motion around the square, vague in the moody light. Our little view for the evening, other than the Burger King that loomed discreetly out of shot.

– Done?

– Yeah.

He snatched his pint and supped gratefully. My stomach felt bloated from the ridiculous portion of mussels and the overdone frites. No more pictures of me that night, I couldn't bear the thought of my belly straining against the soft fabric of my dress.

Leon huffed on his vape, sending out a watermelon scented cloud that seemed completely at odds with our surroundings. How can something so infuriating wind up being so endearing? The sweet, cloying smell of his vape and his actual musk are mingled in my mind, completely inseparable.

***

Next: a shot composed of one-thirds canal and two-thirds dark, empty, cobbled street. Amber light spreads over the cobbles, and pools like chunks of caramel in the black, still water.

– Another drink?

On the other side of the road, German tourists skulled back Guinness outside the Irish bar. An awful racket: laughter and slurred speech and Liam Gallagher whining over the speakers.

– I'm a bit tired actually.

He grinned, his face in silhouette against the streetlamps.

– Let's go.

I felt his hand on the small of my back, and a shiver ran through me despite the heat.

***

Shortly after, his lager-watermelon tongue probed my mouth. His hands gripped my sides hard, his bristles scraped my chin, both our bodies slick with sweat. Panting in time, sinking and rising from the mattress in tandem. Suddenly, his tongue spasmed around my teeth and he collapsed on top of me in a triumphant final thrust.

– Done?

– Yeah.

He smiled sheepishly, sweet all of a sudden. He lurched off me, and within a minute he was quietly snoring.

I lay there, my heartbeat slowly winding down. My body tingled with expectation, but he was pissed: I didn't want him lapping at me like an over-enthusiastic puppy until I pretended to finish.

My finger felt my wetness, and slowly I began to rub.

***

For breakfast, an overhead shot of avocado spread along a lump of crusty sourdough, buttery scrambled eggs on the side. Knife and fork on the right, orange juice on the left.

Leon was already halfway through his açaí bowl, an empty americano beside him.

– Could you not have waited?

He mumbled, mouth half full.

– What?

– I was hungry, babe.

He shrugged.

– I've a hangover that'd floor a horse.

***

Next: he is on the back of the canal boat, arms outstretched along the stern. He's flanked by sun-lit water and ornate, pointy buildings that scratch at the sky.

– How long is this anyway?

– 30 minutes.

– Alri'.

He exhaled a watermelon vape cloud. A red-faced German glared at Leon, arching his bushy grey eyebrows.

Leon offered the vape in response.

***

The gallery: a cheeky shot of Van Eyck's The Virgin and Child with Canon van der Paele painting. The photo doesn't quite capture it: I took it at an awkward angle, and the lighting sort of glares slightly off the canvas. You can't make out the sheer precision of the brushstrokes, the vibrancy of the colours: the green of the parakeet, the saucy red of her cloak, the pure white of the Canon beside her. I'm not good with words. I can't really explain. I suppose I was trying to capture how it made me feel. That's why I broke the rule.

– No photos!

Leon glared at the attendant.

– Sssssh!

– No photos!

– Ssssssh! We're tryin' to enjoy the art.

I squeezed his arm, felt blood rush to my cheeks.

– Sorry, sorry. I won't do it again.

***

More snaps: sunlit squares, shadowy side streets. Frites for lunch. Chocolate drenched waffles for dessert.

***

A deluge of beers: a different one every time, each one in a unique glass. Kriek and Lambic and Tripel and even a Trappist ale.

–I 'd murder a Guinness.

Veins bulged in his arms, after the callisthenics he did back at the hotel. No matter where he is or what he's at, he makes time for exercise.

We were outside the Irish bar. A GAA match had been on: he'd insisted on seeing it. Not my thing, but you have to compromise. You do stuff for him, he'll do stuff for you. I was on my phone, already planning what I'd make him do next. Maybe the Basilica? Or the Belfort?

Meanwhile, Leon was commiserating with the Tyrone crowd.

–Ye got wrecked lads. Wrecked.

– Aye, yer right. That penalty though?

Leon's always making friends.

– Fancy doing the Belfort?

– Ah yeah, babe. When?

– Now? It closes in 45 minutes.

– Ah, I'm halfway through a drink. Tomorrow maybe? There's great craic here.

– I can do it myself?

– If ye like. Meet ya back here?

– Yeah. Someplace else for dinner then maybe?

– Yeah grand, babe. Take loads of pictures.

***

Next: The view from the Belfort. The old city stretches out in the slowly fading light, like a portal right into the past. The last of the sun's light bathes the streets in liquid gold. From the height, all the Burger Kings and knick-knack shops are invisible.

The bells sounded when I was up there. I watched the wires pulled by the rotating drum below, listened to the bells clang and clatter and crash and chime all around me, and I wished there was some way to capture what I felt. The sense of freedom, or like I didn't know where I was, or when I was. The feeling of forgetting. Or something. I don't know.

It ended with a deep, echoing thump.

⁂

Dinner: a 'Flemish' Stew and frites. It looks messy and half-arsed. I omit Leon's cheese string pizza.

– See? It's not too bad.

The beef was rubbery, the sauce thin and over salted. The side salad looked like it came straight out of a packet. I could already feel my stomach prepare a litany of complaints. Eating authentic Belgian cuisine at the Irish Bar… I gazed longingly across the square at the 'Home of the Flame-Grilled Whopper.' Anything would be better than this. I prepared a list of activities that I would force him to do with me the next day. After a night spent traipsing after loud Nordies, I reckoned he owed me.

⁂

Next: Leon grins, surrounded by lads in Tyrone jerseys. It's a good picture. I should know, I took it myself. He's grinning centre-frame, arms draped over his new friends' shoulders. No flash, sort of murky but it feels candid, spontaneous, stylishly blurry.

– Another drink babe?

– Ah no. I'm shattered.

– Mind if I've another?

His constant restlessness really drew me to him. He pulls me out of myself, gets me to go places or do things I'd never do otherwise. At that moment though, all I wanted to do was collapse back at the hotel and rub my swollen stomach.

– Fine.

⁂

More night-time shots: streets that appear desolate, boats gliding lazily on the canal, the tawny glow of the streetlamps against the black of the sky.

– Ah come on, for fuck sake.

– Please, I'm tired.

– Come on. They're headin' to the club. In Bruges. A club in Bruges.

– I'm just too—

– We did your thing all day.

He stared at me, his face in shadow against the amber streets,

– What?

– Photos. Snappin' pictures.

– So?

– So? Now it's my turn.

– Fine. Go on. I'll see ye later.

I walked off, waiting for his hurried footsteps behind me. They failed to materialise.

– Ah here, I can't leave ye walk home alone.

– It's fucking Bruges, Leon.

***

From the album, you'd think we were having a really good time. Sitting here now, drenched in sweat, that spring digging into my back, Leon puking loudly in the ensuite, I nearly half convince myself it was all great fun. Pictures don't lie, or at least they don't appear to unless you took them yourself.

I remember him coming back. Reeking of sweat and stale drink and fags. The clumsy fumble of his cold hands, the warm moistness of his cock digging into my thigh.

– Leave me alone.

He fell back onto his side of the bed. His breathing was ragged. He mumbled something. He burped. Then a second burp, wetter sounding. Then a dry retch. Then, the sound of bare feet smacking the carpet, before slapping the tiles in the ensuite.

***

Now, I'm sitting here waiting for him to toss up his dinner. I don't know why I'm looking at these photos. Maybe I'm looking for some hint of unhappiness.

All I see are some very nice, very tasteful holiday pics.

A sudden splatter. The dry heaves are now wet.

I pick up a glass, and amble to the bathroom. The tiles are cool on my feet.

Leon's bent over the toilet bowl. Naked. His arsehole is staring at me, scrupulously shaven. It quivers redly with each hot retch. I wonder who he shaves it for? A sheen of sweat glares off his limbs. His hands grip the bowl, as if he may suddenly fly off from the force of his regurgitations. The half banjaxed extractor fan stutters, unable to clear the stench of bile and beer and curry sauce.

I place the glass by the sink, and manoeuvre myself so that he is centred in my vision.

I lift my phone.

– Leon?

His red-rimmed eyes gaze over his shoulder. His hair is matted on his forehead in streaky clumps. Greyish ooze glistens on his lips. Tears shine in his eyes. I'm not sure if it's the most intimate thing I've ever seen or the most repulsive. It could be both.

Snap.

At Times I Hear You Calling
Rowe Irvin

2nd Prize, Seán Ó Faoláin International Short Story Competition

Dig a hole. Dig it deep. Deeper. Make a distant circle of the sky. Scoop a hollow, a room. Just wide enough. Tamp the dirt to a floor. Place things on it. A green rug. No, red. Fray its corners, pull its threads. Set a chair, wooden, one leg out of kilter. A porcelain dog, chipped. An enamel basin. Take away the dog.

Put a hook in the wall and on it hang a coat. A heavier coat, one that sags. Rub it through at the elbows. Fade the collar. Twist off the second button. Hang other things on the walls: a decorative plate painted with a heron, a barometer, a cuckoo clock, a cross-stitched scene of horses grazing in a meadow, a framed photograph of a woman, sunlit, squinting. No, take out the photograph, leave the frame empty.

The woman from the photograph, put her on the rug instead. Put her where the light from the sky hits at midday. Set her squatting, head in hands. Leave her there and bring the walls in closer. Straighten her out, stand her up. Tilt her chin to the light, open her mouth. Give her a voice *aaaaaghhhhhhhhhhhhhhhh* no take it back. Brown a few of her teeth, let one molar shrivel away into the gum. Line her face. Grizzle her hair. Pinch up the veins in her hands. Swap one breast for a puckered scar. Stoop her. Stoop her less. Set her walking round the space.

The sky darkens and the hole darkens too. Some other light needed. Try a lamp beside the chair. No, not that. A candle then, in a brass holder. Start it guttering. Pull the woman from her circling and lay her sideways on the rug. Curl her tight. Droop her lids. Fold the rug up and over to stop her shivering. Better still, unhook the heavy coat and drape it across her.

What does she need? Yes, water, fill a jug while she sleeps. An enamel jug, to match the basin. Beside the jug, place a tin. Dent the lid, rust the rim. Drop into the tin a hard rattle of biscuits. Take the decorative heron plate from the wall. Something to put on it. An apple? A green apple, yes. With it a knife, blunt, a hallmark at the base. Now a table for the jug, the plate, the tin. A round table, varnished. No no, not that. Rough the shine from it, scorch it, scuff it, stain it. Give it a tilt. Ring the wooden surface with water marks.

How cramped the room seems now. Dig the walls out wider. Move everything a little further apart. Yes. The room, it pleases. The woman, she sleeps. Wake her with the cuckoo clock before dawn.

She stretches and clicks. She peers at the circle of dark blue far overhead. Her hands tremble in her hair. Bring them down to her sides. Pull her up from the rug, stand her at the table. Wait, bring the chair. Sit her. Let her take the jug and drink from it, long deep swallows. Let her open the tin and shake out three biscuits onto the heron plate, then let her take the knife and hack the apple into chunks. She eats quickly, strewing crumbs. Take away the mess, the apple core. Take the grease of the biscuits from her fingers. Up and set her walking round.

The ring of sky turns pale. Fling open the curtains. Curtains? Yes, brown ones, moth-pocked. Hang them on the dirt wall, over the cross-stitched horses in their meadow. The woman has halted. Set her walking. She halts again. Walk her again. Her water dribbles down her legs and darkens the earth. Okay bring the basin. Tidy what has spilled and move her on.

Later let her rest. When her feet drag let her rest. Head on the table, cheek against the wood. A wind blows into the hole and raises pimples on her skin. Put the coat on her and the pimples flatten out. Take it off and they rise again. Put it on. Take it off. Put it on. Take it off. Put it on. In the coat she stands and gazes upward. The wind sends clouds scudding fast across the opening. There are flecks that might be leaves. Her mouth hangs partway open. Maybe now a voice *aaaagghhhhhhhhhhhhhhh* no quiet her. Stuff her mouth with biscuits instead.

Like this let the days pass. Curl her on the rug, wake her. Fill the biscuit tin and take away her crumbs, her apple cores. One day give her a cheese sandwich. Set her walking, rest her. Empty the basin of her waste. Open and close the curtains on the grazing horses. Light the candle, snuff it. Light it, snuff it. The nights begin to tighten around the circle of the days. The air in the hole cools. Leave the coat on the woman, even as she sleeps. Perhaps now a bed, a heavy thing of black iron, yes. For her head a pillow, an oily stain at its middle. The space wants widening again. Dig and dig until it takes the woman twice the amount of time to walk her circle. Bring back the chipped porcelain dog. Yes, there is room now for that. Put it where the door would be.

It rains. The bottom of the hole slicks to a dark mud. Tuck the woman under the table to keep her dry. She crawls out and kneels in the column of rain that pours through the hole, her face upturned. Pull her back under the table. She crawls out again. She cups her hands to catch the rain. Her hair sticks to her skull. Water runs into the neck of the coat. Pull her back. Again she crawls out to kneel in the downpour. So fetch the table and put it over her. She throws herself at the legs and topples it. Jug, plate and knife go flying into the mud. The biscuit tin opens, spills. So then let her stay. Let her knees clog up with mud. Let the coat soak through. Let the biscuits bloat and come apart.

When the rain stops leave her sodden. Leave her for days and days. Leave the candle unlit, the biscuit tin empty. Let the basin fill and stink. Keep the curtains closed over the horses and their meadow. The woman shivers. She sucks at the mud, at the coat's damp sleeves. The ground dries, hardens. She takes the knife and goes digging for the lost biscuits. She opens her mouth and shouts some silent thing. She watches the sky.

Finally set the table upright. Fill the jug, the tin. No, fill the jug only. Put a hunk of bread on the plate. Mould it, no, only stale it. An apple, bruised and soft. Bring her to the table and sit her on the chair. Let her eat. After, pull the tangles from her hair. Wash the dirt from her knees, her feet. Curl her into the bed. Do this tenderly, tenderly.

Some weeks pass. The woman goes round and round. When it rains she stays put beneath the table. Sometimes in her walking her eyes go to the barometer, to the horses, their green green grass. Sometimes she looks into the empty frame and her brow pleats. She fingers the scar on her chest. In sleeping she twitches. Her jaw moves and she would perhaps speak if *home him with a swing and a clatter in the afternoon singing juniper gentle and rosemary-o clapping the mud from his boots before*—no, none of that. Scuff away the words she scratches into the floor.

Some change needed. A new rug? This one striped. No, change it back. The porcelain dog, move it to sit beside the candle. Yes, that is something. That does well. For a few days that does well. And yet. The coat then, hang it on the opposite wall. No, drape it over the chair. No, put it back where it was. What else? The woman, send her walking round the other way. Move her from chair to bed, chair to bed. Coat on, coat off. For a change, take the *cuh-cooo-cuh-cooo* from the cuckoo clock and replace it with an owlish screech. The first time the woman is woken by its shrilling she jumps up and runs for the curtains as if their drapes concealed a window she might hurl herself through, as if she might go tumbling into the green meadow where the horses bend their heads, as if she might flee barefoot across the grass and feel the dew—whoops! None of that. Press her back into the bed. When she sleeps set the clock screeching again. Again. Sleep, screech, jump. After the twelfth time she no longer reacts, only lies still, her eyes fixed upwards.

Tuck a photograph into the frame, this one of a man. Let her look at it and look at it. Leave her looking. Leave her in her hole. Dig a new hole, to the same depth. Widen it to a room, smaller than hers. The man from the photograph, put him into the second hole. Plump him, sag him. Give him a voice *aggghhhhhhhhhhhhhhh* no best take it back. Fill his hands with biscuits. He eats standing up, his jaw slow.

Between the two holes dig a tunnel. Let the man come to the woman. Let them embrace. Let them stroke each other's cheeks. Let them have days of sky and biscuits. Let them eat sandwiches on fresh white bread. Let them rub together in the bed. The man puts his hand to the scar on the woman's chest; she breathes against his palm.

One night while they are sleeping take the man and put him back into his own hole. Fill the tunnel. Screech the clock. The woman beats on her dirt walls. The man beats on his. Their mouths stretch. Prod the man down into the dirt. Pull the earth back into the second hole. Close it up. Pack it tight.

The woman in her frenzy has smashed the porcelain dog against the barometer. Both the dog and the barometer's glass front are shattered. The thin hands of the barometer dangle loose. The woman stamps and waves her arms. She picks up the dog's porcelain head, a chunk of glass; she fits them jagged in the wall like handholds, footholds, perhaps to climb out of there, perhaps to pull herself over the rim of the hole and stand at last in the sky's wideness, to see trees, to see distance, to stretch out her hands and catch the leaves when they—whoopsie! Take away the pieces of the dog. Take away the broken glass. Take away the table too, and everything on it. Take away the rug, the chair, the bed, the candle. Take away the basin. Take away the coat, leave her bare. Clear the walls, leave them bare.

Gone the horses in their meadow. Gone the cuckoo clock and the man's photograph. Gone the curtains. Gone the heron on its plate. Gone the candleglow. Gone the pillow with its oily stain where their two heads lay.

Dig out the space around the woman. Dig it wider. Wider still. Make it vast and cavernous. Make it so deep that the sky is a needleprick the woman must squint to see. Send her walking from one edge to the other. Cut high ledges into the walls and on them place apples that it takes her days to climb to. Dig a maze of tunnels and set her crawling through. Leave biscuit crumbs at intervals, let her find them. At the centre of the maze put a cheese sandwich. When she reaches it, fold up the tunnels and bring the walls in close again. Closer. Pull them tight around her, so she has to scrunch. The sky is a circle again, directly overhead.

Put a sound in the hole, that of a door opening to the noise of a road, a jangle of keys. Let her listen. A new sound, this of rain against glass. Change it to a man's voice, lilting, some wordless tune. The voice rises and falls. The woman lies still, hands curled in the hollow of her chest. Another sound now, what? Birds, yes, birds. A single steady warble, like the calling of a dawn. The woman smiles. She cranes her neck to see the sky. Drop in more birdcalls. More. Fill the hole with cries and craws. Let them go on and on. Her smile buckles. Her hands cover her ears. Pull them away. Now a new sound, yes, this of fire moving through a forest, trees crackling and bending and breaking, things shrieking and fleeing and dying. Now take the sound away. Take all sound away. Let light and dark pass over her in silence. She breaks a fingernail scratching her words into the dirt. Scuff them out. Close the hole above and take away the sky.

In her darkness, in her hole, the woman is restless. She turns in cramped circles. She seems to be looking for something, feeling into the edges of the hollow, scrabbling about with her hands. Her lips are moving. What is she saying? So give her a voice *home the leaves how they gather in piles under the stoop the rattling door here that slate's blown off again and smashed to bits I'll use the pieces to line the pots and buttering bread for the both of us humming the old tune don't you love the old tunes his one good hip cocked like some crooner's to flick me up from my reading and tilt me giddy like a girl remember this remember da-dee-ah-dee-da-the-month-of-May how we used to how we still dee-daa still got it creaking in step how lovely we were you're lovely still oh tshh it's true and later his hand grimy on my knee in the kitchen we'd sit our two stiff backs and watch the fields rippling beyond the window over the sink the sky the poplars the other week a great folding mass of starlings like a blue-black sheet held out in the wind then two days later a buzzard mobbed by crows must be they've got a nest there I said and him leaning with that rough sparkle I suspect they just do it for a laugh the crafty bastards to which I bend like a stalk the creases in our foreheads he is always catching me like this it's him like always catching me and catching—*

Tell it to the Water
Eamon Doggett

It was less of a river than a stream as it was not wide—it could be crossed with a run and a good jump—and it was not deep—in its middle the water barely reached your shins. Although the odd rock saw it eddy, it flowed steadily and seemed faithful to a noble order. We didn't know much about it: where it was coming from or going. Not that this mattered. The important thing was that it was our stream to watch, to examine, to jump, to bridge.

'Big one here,' Tadhg, my brother, said. He had walked up the gentle bank to the flat and a muddy patch of grass. I watched as he bent his knees, gripped the rock with two hands and lifted it off the ground an inch but no more.

'Let me try,' I said.

'No, I have it,' he said.

We tried to land stones close to the far bank, but sometimes they came up short, or we overshot them, and they missed the water entirely. Often we landed a stone in a good spot, only for it to keel over and end up out of reach. The best sound was when a stone missed all the others and hit the water squarely with a deep kerplunk.

'What do you think?' Tadhg asked.

'A few more—a few gaps still to fill,' I said.

He threw in more stones, and I did the same until we were stood at the stream's edge, ready to shoulder the other out of the way.

'Please,' I said.

I hesitated only momentarily for him to step onto the first stone and plant his body in my way. I wanted to push him into the water, but as he reached halfway across, with his arms outstretched like a tightrope walker, I wanted him to make it. 'Keep going,' I said. He had a wobble in an area that needed more stones—a moment when the water seemed to brace to meet him—but he made it across and looked back at me. I followed, wobbling in the same area, but I made it as well. We walked toward a corridor of bramble bushes which would bear blackberries in a few months. That would be another adventure (jam jars and step ladders), but there was nothing for us for now. So we walked east toward the perimeter of the mobile home park and its pastel-coloured vans. Beyond that were the amusement park, the chipper, the small shops and houses that fringed the dunes and the sea.

'We could go to the shop,' I suggested.

Tadhg didn't respond.

'What do you want to do?'

'I don't know.'

The sky was grey with clouds, and the light was weak. We walked back to the stream and looked at our handiwork, at all the stones of different colours, shapes and sizes that had colonised the water. I imagined fish agitated and dazed as they struggled for a route through the impasse.

'What is pushing it?' I asked.

'What do you mean?'

'Where does it get its momentum?'

'It starts up in a mountain, doesn't it? It's gravity, I guess.'

'But this is all flat around here. Why doesn't it slow to a stop?'

Tadhg stared down at the water.

'Imagine a stream of honey,' I tried. 'It wouldn't move at all, would it?'

'I guess not.'

We took turns walking across our bridge, over and back, hoping one of us would fall into the water. Then, more confident, we went from opposite sides and passed each other halfway across. This turned into a race that eventually saw me lose my footing and dunk a shoe in the water. Tadhg laughed, and I was glad to give him something to laugh about and stave off boredom. I took off my wet sock to dry as Tadhg lobbed stones in the air to land in the water with a splash. The sun had broken through the clouds.

'Why don't we try to stop it?' I suggested.

'What do you mean?'

'Make a dam.'

'You want to try to block the water?'

'Yes.'

Tadhg picked up a stick and started poking at the edges of the stream, disturbing the mud and clouding the water.

'It wouldn't take that many more stones,' I argued. 'It would deepen the water, too.'

'How's that?'

'It's like putting a plug in the bath. If the water has nowhere to go, its level will rise—it will get deeper.

'You think the water is going somewhere?'

'What do you mean? Of course it is.'

'It might not want to go anywhere.'

'It's finding its way back to...' I waved my hands in a vague direction. 'To the sea—it is on its way to the sea.'

Tadhg did not seem satisfied with this explanation. I was losing him.

'Imagine if fish start swimming there,' I said.

He allowed an elaboration.

'If the water deepens, fish could start swimming here. We could have our own fishing spot.'

There was a giddiness in my voice, and I knew Tadhg was also excited by the prospect. But we couldn't be excited at the same time, so he feigned indifference.

'I don't know. It sounds like a lot of effort,' he said. 'I think I'm going to go home. Mum will be wondering where we have gone.'

'Right then.'

'Right then, what?'

'I'll do it myself.'

I knew I had won.

'If we are going to do it,' he said. 'We should get some tools. A bucket to fill with stones.'

'And a shovel,' I said.

'And a rake.'

We walked quickly through the field, part of the farmland surrounding our house on two sides.

On the rare occasions we saw the farmer, he worked alone, carrying a stick to direct his beasts towards a feeding pen of deep, muddy ground. We didn't know whether the cattle were domesticated for meat or milk or simply left to roam.

We climbed the fence into our back garden and reached the shed, but we couldn't grab our tools without our mother hearing.

'What are you two up to?' she asked.

'Nothing.'

'What are you doing in the shed, then?'

'We just need some tools.'

'Tools for what?'

'We are building a dam on the stream.'

'A dam? That's not your stream to be building a dam on.'

'Whose stream is it?'

She thought about this, and when she could not come up with a convincing answer, she told us to be careful, to put on our wellies, and to be back by six o'clock. We were having shepherd's pie for dinner.

With a rake in hand and wellies on his feet, Tadhg walked into the middle of the stream and began to draw stones towards him. I shovelled stones into a bucket and tipped them into the water for him to arrange. We found a steady rhythm, occasionally stopping to admire our progress.

'We are getting there,' I said.

'It's looking good, but the water is still coming through.'

'Just need more stones.'

The dam wall stretched from one side of the bank to the other and had grown about twice the height of the water's original depth. The water level on the upstream side had risen about four inches and turned a shimmering green. The downstream side had become a mere trickle that flowed in thin, silvery threads as it jostled with stones. The more stones I moved, the more my hands and arms seemed to hang lower and further from my sides. It was a good tiredness, and a break felt natural and deserved. I took four biscuits from my pockets and handed Tadhg two. They were crumbling at the edges but retained their shape.

We took turns staring at the stream. When Tadhg stared at it, I turned to look towards the fields, the cows and our house. When I stared at the stream, Tadhg faced another way. He was the one who spotted Gareth, our neighbour, in pale green football shorts and a yellow t-shirt, bouncing a ball as he walked towards us. It was already too late to run away.

'What are you doing?' he shouted.

'Nothing,' I said.

'Are you building something?'

'How did you find us?'

'Your Mum told me you were out here. What are you doing?'

'Nothing.'

'She said you've been out here for hours.'

'So what?'

Gareth looked around him, smirking.

'What are you doing with the bucket?'

'Nothing.'

'Doesn't look like nothing,' he said, motioning to our dam. 'It looks like a bridge. Why do you need all those stones? You could cross it with three or four.'

'It's a dam.'

'A dam? To block the water?'

'Yes.'

'Why do you want to block the water?'

'We want to deepen it.'

'Why?'

'Just because.'

'Because what?'

'Because we want to.'

'Why?'

'We want to fish—'

Tadhg cut me off. 'We want to swim in it,' he said.

'No, what was that about fishing?' Gareth asked. 'You want to fish it? But there's no fish in this stream. How could there be?'

I could feel Tadhg's eyes threatening me, but a part of me wanted to share our theory, to wave our imaginative vision.

'If the dam is tight, the water will deepen upstream,' I said. 'If the water deepens, fish will start to swim in it.'

Gareth looked down at the water, contemplating. Then he threw the ball to Tadhg, who caught it and threw it to me. We tossed the ball around as we talked.

'How do you know fish will appear all of a sudden?' Garth asked.

'We can buy fish eggs.'

'You can buy them?'

'Yes.'

'And what, they will just magically hatch?'

'Yes.'

Gareth rolled his eyes.

One day, he appeared at our house with a new football and a massive bag of jellies. We played outside until dark, and he kept appearing at our house after that, constantly bouncing a ball and eating sweets. He talked a lot. I didn't think it was possible to talk that much.

'I want in on this,' he said.

'What do you mean?'

'If you lads are setting up a private fishing club, I want in on it.'

I looked at Tadhg and saw he shared my concealed excitement. We were the gatekeepers of something special. Our project had been legitimised.

'We have done all the work,' Tadhg said. 'You can't just be in on it. You've only just got here.'

'Don't pretend you are doing anything special. You are just throwing stones in the water.'

To demonstrate, Gareth hurled a stone into the water that clattered off other stones before settling on the dam wall. Tadhg and I looked at each other to intervene as he went for another.

'You can't just randomly throw the stones,' I said.

'Why not?'

'There is a system.'

'What's the system?'

'It's hard to explain.'

'What is it?'

'It's…'

'See! There is no system.'

'You need to put the right stone in the right place,' Tadhg interjected, 'or else there will be gaps between them. It's like a jigsaw puzzle—some stones don't fit together. You need to get the right placement.'

'What can I do then?' Gareth asked.

He was fidgeting with his empty pockets.

'Help me fill up the buckets, then,' I conceded.

With that, we got back to work. I used the shovel to fill the bucket while Gareth gathered stones with his hands. Once the bucket was brimming, we carried it to the stream's edge and launched the stones into the water. Tadhg lifted the stones into place until he could not keep up, and work stalled.

'Let me do it for a bit,' Gareth said. 'You do the bucket for a while.'

Tadhg sighed as he straightened his back and rested his hands on his hips.

'Just for a few minutes,' Gareth tried.

'You've no wellies on.'

'That doesn't matter.'

We watched as Gareth removed his shoes and socks and entered the water. Tadhg joined me on the bank and caught his breath as we watched Gareth begin to pile stones on top of other stones. We let him work for a while before we started on another bucket. The wall grew higher and denser as we rotated between roles. We tried to be the best at every role we undertook, and this competitive spirit sustained our work until Gareth became restless.

'Let's do something else,' he said. 'Let's get our bikes and go to the shop.'

'We are building a dam,' I said.

'Or football? Why don't we go to the estate and see if a match is going on? I'll introduce you to people. I know everyone on the estate. They have big goals there as well.'

'We are fine here,' I said.

'You want to keep doing this all day? Playing with stones?'

'Leave us if you don't want to help.'

'Come on,' he said, stretching his arms wide. 'It's summer—let's do something!'

By now, the dam was tall and wide enough to dominate the stream, becoming the fixture around which the landscape seemed to revolve. I imagined a few more days' work would solidify the structure and ingratiate it with the stream's sensibilities.

'This is pointless,' he said. 'The water is still getting through. You need cement. You can't build a wall without cement.'

'It just needs more stones,' I said.

'It won't make a difference. The water will still find a way through.'

'Leave us to it, then.'

'Shut up with that. Let's do something.'

We ignored him and kept working. Tadhg used the rake to level off the dam's banks and tighten the stones together. Gareth began to sulk as he paced up and down the stream's edge, bouncing the ball as he went.

'I don't like it,' he kept saying.

'What don't you like? I asked, eventually.

'We shouldn't disturb nature like this. It feels wrong. It's in the word *nature*.'

Tadhg and I stopped working to look at Gareth, who stopped bouncing the ball to elaborate.

'The stream, like everything else, has its own nature,' he said. 'It wants to flow; it needs to flow. But we're disrupting it. It's like Adam and Eve—we're disobeying God, we're sinning. He made the stream pure, and now we've... what's the word? Con-tam... con-tam-inated it. We need to put the stones back.'

Tadhg turned to me. 'I think I agree, actually. It's like you said earlier—the stream wants to find its way to the sea. We're bullying it.'

'That's exactly it!' Gareth said.

'It's just a stream,' I argued. 'You're acting like it's a person! We've been working on this for ages, Tadhg.'

I was embarrassed by the desperation in my voice, by my appeal to my younger brother, who only looked down at the stream, causing us to follow his gaze. On the upstream side of the dam, where the water ran deeper, it was dark and inky—a friend of the imagination.

'Did you see that?' I asked, pointing to the water.

'See what?'

'A fish! It was big. I saw a flash of it.'

'A flash of nothing,' Gareth said.

'I swear I saw something.'

'Where?' Tadhg asked, moving beside me to trace the direction of my finger.

'There,' I said.

While Tadhg focused on the spot, Gareth moved to the other side of me to do the same, and we went silent for a few minutes.

'I see it!' Gareth said.

'See, I told you!'

His voice went flat. 'Yes, I see a white horse jumping over the stones.'

'Honestly,' I said. 'I saw something.'

'You only saw what you wanted to see.'

'I saw it,' I said, and I was still arguing my case when Gareth began dismantling the dam, throwing stones off its wall in all directions.

'What are you doing?' I asked, rushing over to him.

'I'm undoing our sins.'

Sections of the wall were collapsing into the water. When one stone fell, another followed. Herds of them were escaping. I wasn't a violent person—I had never been in a proper fight—but I pushed Gareth as hard as I could. In the millisecond he hung in the air, he shrieked giddily before landing heavily on the dam's upstream side, splashing water around him. As he stumbled towards me, I clenched my hands into fists, but his hands were open-palmed, and his wet face was flushed with excitement. 'That's what I'm talking about,' he yelled as he tackled me to the ground. The next thing, we were all wrestling in the water. Tadhg and I tried to pin Gareth down, but he kept wriggling free of our grasp and howling with joy: 'This is it, lads!', 'Now I see you!', 'Mano a mano!'

It ended when Tadhg twisted his ankle when slipping on a rock. Gareth's excitement faded into concern as he helped Tadhg out of the water. We all sat on the bank, our clothes sopping wet, our breaths ragged gasps.

'Mum is going to kill us,' Tadhg said.

'Would you stop,' Gareth said. 'It was a bit of fun.'

I looked at the remains of the dam. Although its function was still apparent, it had lost its integrity; water flowed through the breaches, threatening to undermine the whole structure. The only saving grace was that the raw materials, the hundreds if not thousands of stones we had accumulated, were close at hand. I picked up the shovel and began to feed the dam with more stones. The palms of my hands were sore. It was a jaded few minutes before Gareth found the will to protest.

'Would you just let it be, for Christ's sake,' he said, suddenly tired now.

Tadhg, too, looked unmoved by the idea of resurrecting the dam. He slowly moved his ankle in small circles and held his head back to look at the sun.

I kept working. I tried to hold back water that was joyful now as it sped through cavities in the wall's face. But I was thinking of what Gareth had said about nature, and I wasn't sure if the dam was such a good idea; I felt childish for conceiving it in the first place.

In the distance, amid the soupy light, I could make out the farmer rounding up his cattle with cracks of his stick. He looked tired, too, or I imagined he was, and there were stragglers, cows that weren't following his orders, that had still not gotten their fill of the late afternoon sun. He knew it might be a while before he could secure the corral gate and bring some order to the world.

All in the head

Dillon Jaxx

I was the only one who knew aunt Edith had a bird living in her head. The anticipation would have me take two, three steps at a time in the cabbage scented stairwell to reach her room at the very top of the building. My dad would utter a stiff hello and go and read the paper in the residents' lounge. Mum would be assigned an errand and then aunt Edith would root and rustle in her handbag and press fifty pence into Kevin's palm to buy Maltesers in the tuck shop. When just me and her remained in the room, she patted the bed for me to come sit beside her. She'd turn her head, and with an almost undetectable click unhinge the left side of her skull. The bird was a brutal blue with rain boot yellow feathers and a copper tipped beak. It wore a pair of tiny glasses because, aunt Edith said, of how much time it spent living in the darkness in her head. The bird looked in my direction and fluffed onto my open palm where it brimmed and pipped while aunt Edith gently wiped and dusted the inside of her skull, making sure to replace the bird's knickknacks exactly as she found them. While she did this she would tell me that when the time came I would be the one that would have to take care of the bird, no one else knows, *promise me,* she'd say, when the time comes. I was focussed on the creature in my palm, every time as fascinated as the first, and I didn't know how to tell the time or if it was coming or going. Kevin had a Casio but I was still months away from my seventh birthday when I too would receive a watch. And then one day dad picked me up from school which was usually what mum did, and as we walked home, I had to adjust my steps to his in a walk-run, not really managing to take in the salamanders sunning themselves on my favourite wall. I could tell even before we got in, that the day suddenly smelt different. Dad said we had to be quiet, mum has a sadness. That's how he said it. As though it was a timid pet we weren't to startle, or an idea she shouldn't be distracted from. My breaths started slamming themselves against my throat, running away from me and trying to chase them got me put in bed with a fever. The day of the funeral was my first day out of bed. As we stood outside the church, mum and dad shaking hands with people as they arrived murmuring words I couldn't make out, my good blouse itching my arms and my shiny shoes pinching my feet, I suddenly realised, the time had come. I told mum I was feeling unwell and could I go inside and sit down. Inside the church I started running towards the front, my shoes echoing on the polished floor like god snapping his fingers. I had to stand on tiptoes to see inside the little boat shaped wooden bed, stuffed with shiny slippery cushions and flowers when I realised I was at the wrong side of her face. I walked around and lifted her head ever so gently to find the clasp. Her skin felt cool and plasticky and I didn't like it.

I'm sorry I'm late, I whispered. I undid the side of her head and bent down to look for the bird. There were all its knickknacks packed in boxes, his glasses folded and placed on top but no sign of him. *Aunt Edith,* I said, *I'm here, I'm here to take care of the bird,* tears rolling down my face. As I was closing the flap I found one tiny feather. Rain boot yellow and a blue that made me long for things as yet unknown to me. I picked it up, enclosing it in my fist tightly, just as I heard the huge church doors groan open.

I was confined to bed for nearly a year. In and out of hospitals for tests, in and out of fevers. On my seventh birthday dad carried me downstairs. Mum had bought me new pyjamas. We sat at the table, they sang happy birthday trying not to sound sad, and we ate slices of poppyseed cake and drank chilled almond milk. I unwrapped my presents, a notebook and lemon scented pen from Kevin and of course, a watch from mum and dad. That night my temperature soared. Mum slept on a chair in my room, creeping out to the bathroom to refresh my flannel all night long. I had a dream-memory of mum asking me not to die, I had a dream-memory of Kevin stroking my face, whispering something into my ear, all night long I was in and out of sleep and dreams. The following morning, something felt different. Mum was asleep in the chair, her skin white, her eyes red and swollen. I went out into the bathroom, my legs feeling like my old legs, not wobbly or weak. I looked into the bathroom mirror, searching my face for clues. I turned to one side then the other, when I noticed something on the left side of my face, just by my ear. I went to touch it, it was hard, but I had seen a scab like this before. And then, my fingers working automatically, I opened the clasp turning my head to see in the mirror. Wearing his perfect tiny glasses, rain boot yellow feathers, impossibly blue chest, like a tiny proud thumb, there he was, blinking at the light shining in from the day breaking into the bathroom just as Kevin knocked on the door telling me to hurry, I had a watch now, did I still not know what time it was.

Great as Anything

Zoë Meager

'I can't sleep,' says the girl.

'Then just close your eyes and stop talking,' says her mother.

They have driven through flooded roads, deeper than the woman dared. The way she had to keep pushing them further into a night that only got meaner and more unhinged. It made her sing songs from *Mamma Mia!* just to cut the tension, until her daughter put her hands over her ears and screamed. Still the wind screamed louder.

In the end though, when their little car was sent skidding across the centre line by punch after punch of wind, and the headlights were no more use than candles, they'd had to pull over.

They kicked their wet sneakers aside and peeled off their socks, flung raincoats into the backseat. Now all they're left in are thin cotton dresses, wet through. The woman knows they shouldn't fall asleep in wet clothes but boy is she too tired to care right now, and in the car it's hot as a rainforest burning. She sweeps droplets off her arms and legs, wipes her hands down her dress, pulls the hem up and presses it to her forehead. Doesn't matter anymore what's rain and what's sweat.

From the boot comes a muffled meow, and even he sounds defeated.

For a week without relief the sad water darkened every window in the city. The sky served only variations of grey; the heavens full of weekday dinners.

Hours, days went by, then three nights ago, the weather turned on them completely.

The woman stood at the window and witnessed the collapse. Sometimes there was scatty lightning and serious thunder, or clouds outlined in random colours: gold, purple, green. Everywhere, wet fronds nodded and shook at the same time, unsure and disagreeing, and the birds hid, who knows where.

Wind leaned on the house like a drunk at the end of the night, incoherent shouting, and strange objects were seen tumbling down the street: sheets of plastic from construction sites, torn branches, rubbish bins and cardboard boxes. The world gone suddenly punk.

The radio played constantly, and the woman nodded as it told her not to worry about the spring bulbs being drowned, or the residents of rest homes because they were taking care of their own, apparently. Her attention drifted in and out, interrupted by the static in her head and quick searches on her phone for *windows open cyclone?* and *lights flickering storm?*

She paced the musty rooms. Went back to the window and tried to believe it. Tried to make out the neighbours' houses behind the blurring rain.

Occasionally, the girl padded out of her room to glance out the window and then look up at her mum. She clutched the soft toy rabbit untouched since she was eight, when his eyes had popped off in the wash and been sewn back on quite crooked. Ever since, he'd expressed a kind of world-weary hysteria.

The girl has studied climate collapse for her whole school life. Done a special project about habitat loss in sub-Antarctic regions, designed a poster about water consumption in recycling, written essays about renewable energy and developing nations. Already encyclopaedic.

Now flood waters rushed like a broken promise down the street. The nearby river burst its banks, and they stood together, mother and child, witnesses with the faces of drowning fish.

'Should we go, Mum?'

The river they'd always known for its transparency—the stony fish, the beer cans and the ducklings—had spun around pubescent, saying *I hate you! You can't tell me what to do!*

The woman kept herself pointed at the glass, eyes open, while the river rushed down to brood in a deep pool of itself at the far end of the street. Neighbours down there were clearing out, stopping to bang on doors along the way. Everyone down there was very small, though, and the water too seemed very far off, or perhaps not real at all.

'Mum? Should we go, Mum?'

A man waded through water up to his bum carrying a large bundled figure to a car. His father perhaps, she squinted, or maybe an adult son.

A few houses further down, a red car was picked up and shifted pointlessly by the water, no one inside.

Closer to them, a woman ran barefoot up the middle of the street, squinting against the mess of rain, her arms stretched helplessly after a small white dog. It snapped its head at her and yapped, annoyed at her for not enthusing in the game. How it waved and waved the little drowned flag of its tail.

She charged around the house in a sweat. Yes. Time for final checks. Yes, yes!

With difficulty, rolled two large rugs and heaved them onto the dining table. Boxed her nana's chittering tea set and set it on top of the bookcase. Upended the stools and banged them down on top of the breakfast bar. Dragged a favourite antique armchair on top of her bed. Stood staring at the lounge, the funny things she'd put together to make a home.

Time to finish loading the car. Time to hurry out the door. Take a deep breath and drive away. For the last time ever, could be.

She just needed a moment to dig out folders of the girl's drawings and on her tiptoes, shove them onto the top pantry shelf, in among the unopened packets of vermicelli and lentils.

The girl ran into the kitchen, a rubbish bag full of teddy bears bumping behind her.

'Is the bloody cat in its carrier yet?' The woman said.

'Nah, he doesn't want to.' The girl swung the bag of toys around her in wild circles. 'Just scoop him up and push.'

The woman caught the bag of toys mid-swing and climbed onto the kitchen bench and stuffed them into the alcove above the pantry, shunting them through the whore's fluff and cooking grease.

Below, the girl jittered over the lino in her socks, performing a K-Pop dance in double-time.

The woman's phone interrupted with an aggressive buzz on the bench and the girl slid over to it. 'It says Tenancy Manager Tracy. Should I answer it?'

'I have to turn the power off next, so don't get a fright.'

The phone buzzed on, heading for the edge of the bench as the girl danced in ever-nervous circles. 'Should I answer it, Mum?' She held her hands in a heart shape, shook a hip, and winked.

'Give it here. Put the cat in its thing! Hello?'

The girl slid away across the lino, passing the empty cat carrier in the hall. 'Some neighbour's at the door or something,' she called over her shoulder.

Along with the cat in his carrier, the boot and backseat are now clogged with: a slab of bottled water, torches, spare batteries, boxes of muesli bars, a wind-up radio, a pillow each, a sleeping bag each, some instant soup mix, cans of beans, a first aid kit with dozens of electrolyte sachets, their family photo albums, their laptops, cat food, the woman's jewellery scrambled together in a shoebox, the porcelain clock she'd inherited from her grandmother, a can opener, toilet paper, a pack of cards, and a backpack each with their passports, birth certificates, medications, and changes of clothes. And she has her handbag and a bunch of grapes. Was there anything they forgot?

There's some cash stuffed into the back of the glovebox too, because the radio recommended it, though the woman is unsure exactly what they'll do with cash.

'Do I have to close my eyes?'

'Look, you've had enough stimulation today. You need to tell your mind to switch off.'

The woman reclines the driver's seat a bit further and curls onto her side, her back rounded towards the girl. Her hands under her head form a cranky pillow.

Debris caught in the wind scours the car and still the rain doesn't stop. Even now it empties over them like a bag of black and white rice.

'It's too stuffy.'

'I know.'

'Can we have the window down a bit?'

'What? No.'

'Because of the rain?'

'It's hardly raining. This isn't what they call real rain. It's just a bit wet.'

They are going to be fine, she knows it. She's done everything right, crossed off every item on her preparedness checklist, followed every recommendation to the letter, obeyed the radio when it told them: to stay home, not panic buy, check on their neighbours, secure large garden items, stay away from windows, keep up-to-date with the latest, save their phone battery, call 111 only if life is at risk, leave everything behind and evacuate their suburb, taking only the essentials.

The woman has stepped her daughter through the official guidance too, involved her, helped her feel in control. She and her tween have been functioning as this neat little team of two and they are going to be just fine.

'It's so stuffy in here I'm going to kill myself,' the girl says.

'You are not. I've already paid your school fees for next term. You'll have to kill somebody else.'

'You?' The girl presses her palm hard into the woman's back, like she could push right through her heart and out the other side, if she liked.

'Kill the sodding mayor if you have to kill someone.'

'Fine, I'll kill the sodding mayor.'

Only after a human body was drawn dead from a culvert across town had the mayor decided to fly back from his holiday home in Fiji. He would have come sooner, he told them over the radio, but his secretary had been unable to book him business class, and, and, and this was probably what ordinary New Zealanders didn't understand: he *had* to be able to work in transit.

'My phone's nearly dead,' says the girl.

'What have you been doing on it?'

'Nothing! *You* said there'd be somewhere charge it.'

'Turn it off for now at least. There'll be outlets in the morning when we get there.'

The woman knows she'll never sleep now. Won't even doze. If she did, the weather would only tangle in her dreams like bad laundry. All single socks.

She uses her fist to smudge a circle in the foggy car window.

In the end, they'd pulled over beside a neighbourhood park, the suburban kind that's no more than a grassed vacancy between houses. She's been past a few times in daylight hours: a broken tetherball and a set of swings, perhaps? Now all she can see is a streetlight dropping its pale orange lozenge onto the mucky green surrounds, and beyond that, an uncertainty of trees that shake delirious, sleepers who want rousing from a rough dream.

The water that encircles the car is rippled with light and dimpled by rain. In an upbeat moment, she would describe it to her daughter as *surface flooding* or *a really great big giant puddle*. The car has a little rise in the road to perch on, with only a metre perhaps on the driver's side where she could step out with any confidence.

She's considered wading to one of the dark houses nearby and knocking on their door, but it's no good: too late, too wet. Dangerous probably. The two of them will just wait things out here on their small island beside the park.

On the dashboard, the girl's phone bleeps and lights up. Its glow is doubled in the windscreen, forming a brief modernist butterfly.

'Who keeps texting you anyway?'

'Suzanne.'

'And how are she and your Dad getting along? They'll be alright in the apartment.'

'Penthouse.'

'They'll be alright in the *penthouse*.'

'Suzanne's got a mother and daughter from out west staying in the spare room. Off Facebook. She's so cool.'

'Of course she has. That's very~!' The woman half-shouts the last word but has to strangle the sentence before the end. She can only say the word *nice* so many times a day before it turns into a hiss.

The girl wriggles. Presses her finger into the soft of her mum's upper arm. 'What if the water gets in the car?'

'It won't.'

'What?'

'It won't!' They're both shouting now, in a squabble with the wind and rain.

The woman tries to stretch her legs, but they've got nowhere to go. She's sore from days of hauling outdoor furniture and pot plants into the garage, drained from lifting everything that was actually far too heavy for her to lift on her own.

She closes her eyes, and the water is there, pouring a steady rhythm over them in the darkness. Better not think of all those radio words like: *surrounded, cut off, engulfed, tragically, swept away, the bodies of two more cyclone victims remain unidentified.* Better think happy thoughts: a clear morning sky, the local marae, hot soup and tea and biscuits.

The woman knows their home by now might be ruined beyond repair. That's a fact. The water could be surging over the front door step, swelling over the couch, washing up the bed legs and the kitchen cabinets. She can't really imagine it, but she tries to, and then forces herself to stop.

She starts the car and cracks the window an inch. A slim rectangle of night looks at her directly and the wall of sound increases, swallowing every thought.

Her daughter is perhaps ignoring her, perhaps starting a collapse into sleep. The girl's small enough to be curled sideways, hugging her knees, and still have room for a drink bottle and the soft toy rabbit beside her on the seat. The woman raises her hand, gently rests her palm on the girl's back. Steady. Asleep.

She shifts carefully back to face her window. Rain indelicately enters the car. It lands on her hands and in her lap, making them shine in the low light. New again, she thinks. Lifts her face to the gap. A coolness, the world's breath on her face. She dissolves into darkness. Thinks back to the white dog running into the storm, the spry package of its body raucous in the face of disaster.

She remembers then, and taps the button to lower the window an inch on the passenger side, then turns off the car.

In Wanting Wanting

Kosoluchi Agboanike

after The Princess (2024)

The man whose concubine I am
has a wife and child.
The child a delight, she, fireworks.
Today, he carries her home on his
shoulder, kicking and cursing; she, fishermen's
bar on his shoulder.
Today, she fires bullets at him. Romance between
lovers, she says.
She, fireworks. His fingers burnt.
But he goes in to her at night.
My bed arctics.
The faithful concubine. I venture an ask,
but his mind is full of her troubles. Always.
Tonight, they fight. She, fireworks, bullets.
He, romance between lovers of fingers burnt.
I think she will kill him. Man
whose concubine I am, but he drinks, fishermen's
bar on his mind.
I venture an ask, the coming in to me of tonight. I am
a woman that wants wanting.
Burnt fingers drink a bar. My bed
arctics.
He comes in to me, smokes bullets, he,
fireworks.
The man with his thinks, and they are plenty.
He smiles at me. The bed arctics,
still.
She, fireworks. His mind burns, still.

Oink

Dean Browne

We were so poor we fried eggs on a spoon.

I held it steady over the candleflame in a cupboard sublet by the butcher.

First of the month he clomped upstairs, eye ringed like the bottom of a coffee cup.

One day he pulled from his apron a pig's ear, for me to play with.

My mother bit her nails back to the elbow.

I pressed it to the floor. I pressed it to the wall. I didn't need a boost to press it to the ceiling.

Mind now, the mother laughed with her nerves.

But I was happy snouting in spider webs and old scrunched-up bills, bills, bills. A smell of wild thyme. I ploughed a furrow in rubbish hunting for truffles.

I couldn't hear her anymore.

I was strung up by my trotters. The room grew smaller, shrunk to a fly's bloody footprint. My backbone cried with the weight of me. Sawdust.

An enamel bucket   blubbed.

The butcher tickled under my chin, *poor child,* just where the wound was.

Back North

Eithne Carson

A cold moon in a clear sky, trees stretching jagged dark arms around the city hall.
Leave in the morning when only the chain cafés are open, trucks unloading outside half lit shops,
Come home in the evening, the city sleeps early, holds onto the curfew it was given in its rebellious youth.
Only restaurants, bars and buses glow after six.
The wide green river down south is a mirror to miles of life, a light polluted sky.
There are parts of Belfast where I can almost see the stars.
The house I go back to is old and tall and cold, its neighbour is haunted, fences barricaded and grown over with vines next to the red brick with its warm windows, reels and radio waves spilling through the cracks in the old stone.
This haunted house is a shadow growing. I tell my friend as she drops me at the door, laughing over the crackling of sparks shot high.
Is that why the children didn't knock this Halloween?
No. I've forgotten what it's like to be young.
All we wanted was to go to the depths of hell and make it out to tell the greatly exaggerated tale.
I try to make the accent fit in my mouth but it feels like a parody.
My father's voice slips back into Belfast every time he crosses the border, even decades later.
I wake up in Winter and I am clean cut and young and I know nothing of the shoes this road has worn down before.
I feel like a Victorian lady when I walk through the dim alleyways, ashamed to take her gloves off to count change for the beggar woman, to see their hands next to each other and recognise the difference between someone who has lived and someone who has survived.
Every wound is fresh and it's one after the other.
I wait for the day I will be nothing but tough skin, and I can take my gloves off with a pride that the way I hold my shoulders or sprinkle stories into my speech tells the world I've seen things.

Colic

Pratibha Castle

At what age did I nudge my mother
off the pedestal of holy

oust her from the role
of roast potato mistress

slam the door shut
on her milk dough cheeks

toe cap of my hobnail boot
shod with gibes   her lemur eyes

fabled windows to the soul
curtainless   persisting in

bleeding bloodless tears
what drove me to sling words

bone blade daggers at a woman
taken   fourteen   out of school

to boil tail clouts in a copper
swaddle the latest sibling

in forgiving arms   cradle
his colic screams in the hour of bats

why shoot her with my smart school
learning   off a wind shiver

branch of rowan   for a
famine of words

Setting the Spuds

Eithne Cavanagh

Potatoes cleanse the soil, you often claimed,
but no crop could clear away the shards
that chimed their tunes against your spade.

I was five and helping you to carve
a furrow by pulling taut a dowel and string.
You let me set my own few spuds and crispy chard.

My little job became an unconscious tuning-in
to ancestral harvest for the fold
long before I ever heard of hunter gathering

Muddy red wellies, my hair uncombed,
I saw you swing spade-weights of soil as if a pendulum.
Sunshine washed your spade shaft with pure gold

its metal scoopblade gleamed like tantalum.
Always clean your tools, you'd murmur,
sharp stone between forefinger and your thumb

A versatile vegetable gardener,
you were happiest in an outdoor space
passing horticultural lore to your only daughter

who, oblivious to her time and place,
learnt contentment from your ways of grace.

It Will Take at Least Five Years to Clear Mines from the Black and Azov Seas

Polina Cosgrave

February is my third spouse. It comes and goes as all things white,
confident in their infinity. Its lies are slow like snowflakes,
but the truth is always momentary. A blinding flash in a foreign sky.
A granite stone in my solar plexus, it means we're married now.

I come from the country of the numb, so I have to be everywhere
to be heard. My language – a split personality, foaming at its lips.
A mother talks of the daily suicides in the army barracks as a routine.
A father says it's not as bad as the journalists claim, they only shelled a street or two.

Our honeymoon: winter in your head.
You're walking along empty explosive-laden beaches mined with the last hope for peace.
The Black Sea licking, licking your heels off,
all the way to the bones.

A Prayer to the One

John F. Deane

> *"I have given them the glory that you gave me,*
> *that they may be one as we are one—*
> *I in them and you in me—so that they may be brought*
> *to complete unity. Then the world will know that you*
> *have sent me and have loved them even as you have loved me."*
> *(John 17:22)*

I

Seeking peace, I was on the island; world in turmoil,
and I, agitated, was still finding sleep
elusive. And so –

morning, still dark, I entered the prayer room, shut the door,
settled myself, to ease towards stillness;
but my mind was a cove cluttered with flotsam

where the sea came pounding, and withdrawing. You
not to be found. I went out onto the foreshore,
yielding; in pre-dawn dimness – a sickle moon,

for here, at the edge, a late spring day may dawn,
unwilling. I climbed over a bulwark of piled boulders
onto the strand, a winter chill still holding,

tide-water shivering in the breezes; out and out
the immeasurable Atlantic and in the far distance
the shapes of islands, like shadows. I walked, hoping still

that You, source and sustenance, might touch my being
to understanding. Here I could avoid the allure of traffic
out on the road, perhaps suppress those iterating whispers

under familiar skies… but I could not avoid
the images of opulence in that far-off white
mansion where, in the Oval office with its fool's gold,

the schoolyard bully, bottom of the class, hunched –
in expanding ego – at the Resolute desk, scrawls his signature,
creepy lines, like a concertinaed serpent, 'executive orders'

for the ethnic cleansing of Gaza, designing mischief
on the poor and the oppressed… but oh! Just One, I cannot
bear it. Listen! those are the cries of gull and guillemot,

a harsh and natural music, beautiful… I shrugged
my defeated spirit deeper into my coat, tried again
to find the stillness deep within. Mercy, I prayed,

on this ageing flesh still stirring, sighing, Divine Breath,
before You, the long-loved beach stretching in a sweet
delaying curve before me, gullies and streamlets crossing

from the sandy-banks to the sea. I stood, listening
to the soothing irregular breaking of the waves;
in the distant barking of a small dog, the bleating of sheep

on the heather slopes of the mountain, I would discern
Your voice; Divine One, I would hold You in a heart of love
but I am fickle as the froth on the wind-swept waves.

II

I know that You, Merciful One, were watching
me, slight and insignificant figure
as I moved along the beach, under the immensity
of sky and sea and mountain range;

I was enthralled by the flight of a tern
out over the sea, small gracious bird, its deadly
arrow-flash of white into the sea,
then flight again, a small life squirming

in its blood-red bill. Gentle One, I have prayed,
pleaded, begged, for the children of Gaza,

for the mothers, for the ragged
unhoused families, with nowhere left to run,

and I have wept, as if You are not listening.
See, here, by the cliffs, the Cathedral Rocks
have collapsed upon themselves, arches and columns
crashed like the rugged faith of old, but this

is in the nature of a cosmic compulsion: the ruins lie,
washed by the waves
and crustaceans cover them; but in Gaza,
Israel's steel-souled cruelty has razed the homes

of the innocent and guilty, a bloody devastation
I thought that we, begotten
of light, had left to the darkness of ages,
this pillage and razing, for the war thunder has been

raking through the psalms, obliterating
the Song of Songs. Forgive me – but ours is an age
of a self-seeking brutality, and I cannot
bear it. You saw how I knelt on the sand, a stench

lifting where I knelt, there were flies, their backs
an emerald incandescence, buzzing noisily
on the manifold kelp and seaweeds rotting in the long
staggering line that marks high tide. I made a poem once,

and wrote: *let the children play,* but now I see
so many, eyes dead, they bleed, they root –
with the dogs, amongst the rubble; I thought of the Child,
who fled from an earlier and more inept Herod

into Egypt. Let the children play, let them breathe
with the sea-thrift blooming on the cliff ledge, but let us not
forget the genocide in Gaza and the West Bank.
I cannot – Gentle One – I cannot bear it.

III

I watched a while, out over the wild and bewildering
Atlantic; on the horizon the islands
rose clearer in the brightening day, and out beyond
our world, the vast and incomprehensible cosmos – and we,
specks of dust, innumerable; where I stood, here
by the cliffs – there is a high bank of sand and sward
eroded by the centuries, guarding the secret graves
of the stillborn and unbaptized, children whose eyes
never opened on a world that had rejected them; Elohim,
we are, before our birth, a nothingness, waiting
in some ocean of pre-existence, waiting til we are washed,
at last, into life; we grow through our deeps and shallows,
suffer the little deaths, and are swept back into silence,
bearing our fardels of being and grace, part of it, portion
of the wholeness, for You will gather all things
into Yourself and nothing will have been lost.

IV

I walked on, more slowly, the sun being risen;
now I had reached the cliffs, gazed up in awe

at those dark, commanding faces. At their feet, somewhat
daunted, I felt alone in the world, the world alone in me;

I would empty my mind of sorrows, into the salt purity
of the air, where I am but one grace-note in the symphony

of growth around me, seeking to discern
that still small voice within the works of love. Then

I remembered that out there, beyond the islands,
there is another predator, part of it, too: the suave

Kremlin vampire, found guilty of war crimes, crimes
against humanity; I see him glide, bat-like, through those

high doors of fool's gold, pugnacious, dwarfed in being
by his greed for domination, thug and ageless backyard bully…

but again, Beloved, forgive me, I fail in patience, and beg
for the mercy You have promised us. I touched

the cold face of the cliffs, inhaled the soft breathing
of cosmos, the now of eternal You, and prayed You

hear me, in spite of sin and dust, faint-heartedness
and fear; I have wearied myself with an awareness

of the horrors of war, the suffering of the children;
oh You, who are nothing and nowhere, intimate and distant,

You who are all in all, and everywhere, Silent One –
I cannot bear it; teach me to pray, teach me trust:

Amen, amen, I cried out, oh Christ our Christ, amen.

Intersection of Francuska and Braće Jugovića

Ajla Dizdarević

On the corner by a kiosk, a pregnant woman holds a baby like a Kalashnikov. Meticulous rags draped over her head tickle the baby's nose. In the light, she looks like a starlet from the Golden Age: strong chin poking through colorful cloth, rosebud lips drying in the sun. Her daily routine: a dinar for the baby she displays like a diorama. A compliment for a coin. When I walk by, she juts the kid out to me for some kiss or a blessing, says the flyaways of my hair look a wondrous halo in the light. *Lady,* I say, *I've never even been baptized.* She jolts the baby around, trying to situate it in my arms, and the thing almost slips out its blanket and onto the ground. I want to sit the woman down, cross-legged, model how I hold even stray puppies tight to my chest a few centimeters from the dirt. But a nearby dumpster fills my sinuses and the heat is getting to me. I push by, my pockets as heavy as they were when I left home. Her child, dawned in a metropolitan manger, is set softly in casings of cockroach shells and pigeon droppings.

From Audley Place

John FitzGerald

See, here is how a city's meant to be. Perfect
in first light, the streets still quiet, redbrick
fronts mirrored in a somnambulant river,
the air expectant *and* replete, another day ahead
of work and sex and death, a confidence of
commerce and prosperity... His dog, attentive
to departure, change in gait or tone. But,
soon he would resume:...There, that spire,

St Mary's, and beyond, the woods of Sunday's Well —
no painter could do justice to. He paused again,
and then the sunlit hills around us seemed
to rise like golden loaves, and the whole scene,
this cradled city, its rooves and labyrinth of streets
and gilded waterways, by now, a miracle.

This Poem

Nicola Geddes

is not living the dream
and has never once been photographed
on a yacht at sunset with a banana daiquiri

This poem will not arouse desire in the over 50s
nor will it be published in *The Stinging Fly*
This poem commits a crime
its words rhyme – but not all the time
It will not be supported by the Arts Council

This poem's mother will fail to be proud
There will be omissions and evasions
until the lack of expected response
slumps between them
like a dead dog in a bin bag

This poem will not be read by Vladimir Putin
He will not recall these words
as he lies in his four-poster bed
silky duvet tucked under his chin
His little eyes gaze up into darkness
not seeing this poem
not feeling its fingers reach his face
pinch his nose, cover his mouth
Rest there

This poem insists on being written at 4:30am
By daylight, it will be gone
The Russian generals and high-ranking officials
will learn of Putin's death with genuine shock
their large jowls
sinking into their square, bemedalled torsos

In the coming hours and days
they will eye each other
with a mixture of suspicion and heavily veiled relief
never realising that this poem
could turn the course of nations

effortlessly.

Chestnut Chapel

Jake M.M. Griffin

How meadows hide their choirs
How woodlouse stride and clovers tower

Rings of oak denote steeple
A clearing is a grove-cathedral

Where subtle touch means tremble
Lips are gospel and pulses rumble

'Lover' translates: apostle
Clad in naught but chestnut and hazel

I will lead, I will follow
Sermons under sun plunging lower

Seeking tide, making harbour
Sending hearts to sink, sink like anchor

Diagnosis

Emilie Jelinek

The patient's jaw is detached: note
how her words have disconnected
from one another, wads of sound stuck
around her teeth, soldering the back

of the throat. Did this disarticulation
happen while eating, laughing, or during
a dental procedure? The medics examine
her lower jaw, enquire whether it is all

in her head. They may do an X-ray to gauge
the gap between her skull base and temporo-
mandibular joint, that is to say the map
of her voice and the silence it must inhabit.

They may ask whether it happened
at New Year's when she was sixteen.
Had her brother wanted to go out
with friends? Had her father not liked

that? Maybe they will ask how he reacted
when her brother dared, at last,
to answer back. Was he was pushed,
did something in him finally snap?

Did he call her father a *fucking dick*?
Medics may ask if this was the comment
that became the trigger that swung the fist
again and again into her brother, then round

into her face when she tried to pry
him loose. They may attempt manual
reduction, where the jawbone is gently
moved back into place. They gently push

the jaw back to where it belongs.
It all happens so very gently, and the words
should flow back as if they had always
been there, as if words could ever rectify

the cross-bite of his moods. A dislocated jaw
is an emergency. Medics can treat it
with reduction if they are able to do it right
away, that is, if she goes to see one. She may

decide not to, may worry about the consequences.
She may be unable to speak to anyone
about the incident on New Year's Eve.
Besides, a medic may agree it is not always

possible to prevent dislocation. The patient
may not be able to avoid all the situations
in which it can happen, such as a car accident
or her father losing it. Sometimes, it takes months

to heal, sometimes it clicks back in place,
sometimes it stays like that for years,
sometimes years can transfigure the moment
that wakes her, still: her father, his hand, her face.

How to Sit on a Man

Kasimma

That's what we're telling you. The Moon, a gulp away from sinking into the stomach of Sky; Earth, a whiff away from sunlight. Children-of-Bird cant with Forest Sticks; Spirits, our venerable audience. Sand, as red as blood in water, chants the irk in the women's feet, trails their train. Their milk-springs slap their belly senseless.

Nwoye's compound is quiet. Nwoye has removed his cloth, reverting to what he truly is + will always be. Entrance—heap of disturbed land where Nwoye's cloth, which caskets his stiff organs, is coffined + planted. Right—where the women will cook if need be. Left—where they'll piss + shit if need be. Front—their camp. Up the ceiling—where we land, our nails scratching the zinc roof, separating dirt from food, our mouths harnessing what feed the spirits left us.

Nwoye jebelụ ife. The women gather in their camp + summon thick spit from the depths of their throats, watery spit from under their tongues. They donate generously, the spit; form a puddle, of spit. They break into shouts of songs, clanging spoons on gourds, pestles on trunks, palm on palm. Calling on Nwoye.

Nwoye's-mother's-girl-child answers. Should she bring them food? The women sing. Calling on Nwoye.

Nwoye's mother answers. If her fellow women would cover their nakedness. Is like she wants to see it all: should they show her: the soft hairs down there: shame did not follow them to come: if Nwoye is not brought to them, the-main-the-main would see the rising Sun. The women sing. Calling on Nwoye.

Nwoye's-mother's-boy-child answers. Nwoye jebelụ ife. Nwoye went on something. They would wait until Nwoye returns: time did not follow them to come. Is there anything he could do on Nwoye's behalf since he's not here?

Fine:

Since he asked nicely: get back inside: produce Nwoye's wife: get them Nwoye's children: make sure all their body parts are accounted for: this house would join Nwoye: if Nwoye's wife + children: don't appear here: before this spit community dries.

Nwoye's wife is brought. Her face shines from tears of grief + from fear of sleepless nights with Nwoye's cloth. She reeks of decay, from spending days with what used to be Nwoye. Her head reflects the rising Sun. Her children cry. The women carry the children. They strip Nwoye's wife of her black raiment + fling it on Nwoye's people. They cover Nwoye's wife with their garment. They dust their buttocks, their legs. They leave their spits behind. They leave. In shouts of songs.

We follow.

香烟烟雾

Emily Anna King 锡萍芳

to the man who smokes a box of cigarettes a day —
do poems by neruda still move you

as embers dim behind your ribcage,
a flare of grief for the rusted town

do you remember nights spent scavenging
through broken glass, and scratched records
for nickels and young people like you

who wanted to travel farther than the telephone wires,
sounds of geese leaving the border, towards lands
made of snow and sand and ivy that climbed
near the seashore,

over spines of books above a
fireplace with three kids, parents and a dog
huddled together reciting the soft places from
where they came

far from harsh vowels and beer — song,
and the hand that grabbed your hand
and brought you to the supermarket,
and the arcades and the bars, and the
woman with a smile so sincere

it was too late in those days for you
to understand she didn't want a cigarette
or your cynicism; my love she wanted who
you were before you met her to join the man
that you are

by the ferris wheel
and the river
and the townspeople with spun sugar
and only a few more dollars in their pockets

and as smoke drifted from your mouth and lines
etched your face and scraps of paper until they made words
you breathed and choked and coughed

and the poems buried deep inside your memory
rose to the surface

on the night you told her
on the night she left
because her train was at 2
        and it had nothing to do with you
        standing there, wondering what she thought of a shameless spirit,
        charring totality, salt in a droplet

Welsh / Not Welsh

Kapu Lewis

Cymreag
starts in the belly
rises to the chest
lungs tug air
of waxy sheep
wool fermented
estuary mud
broken crab
legs scratched
by black heg
branches of
dad's yellowed
Maginogi paperback
read by the hearth
drawn in the soot
surging into parched
mouth ex spelling
a love song
a need
a rhetorical
meaning rounded
as a cowrie shell
contains this spirit

is a tongue
I cut it out
I spat the
key for
the lock in
the door in
the lake in
the mountain in
the maes for
butchered songs of
Pwyll and
Branwen and
Manawydan and
Math and
a melltith of
modern life
clinging to
cliffs as
the sea
erodes this
final outpost
pushed

Notes:
The Mabinogion is a book of Welsh myths – it has four branches following the stories of Pwyll, Branwen, Manawydan and Math.
Mellltith means 'lie' in Welsh.

Axe

Aoife Lyall

You tell me you are carving a new handle
for an axe, replacing an original too damaged
to be saved
          and how you closed your eyes, chose
the wood by weight, by touch, how you held
the blade to skim the bark;
                              how you couldn't help
but breathe the smoke from birch leaves etched
in fire, or from the ash-tipped wolf's pelt
          you scorched while others slept.
There is a poem in here, in this
          thing you made by hand and let me hold
          in mine; in how it could be used to build
or fell an empire. Or both.
                              This could be both.

At the first sex party I go to

Simon Maddrell

I spend the whole time in the kitchen
having arrived with a pocketful of rubber

when my assumed one-on-one disappears
to join whatever-number-some play in the lounge.

I am sucked into the kitchen by a naked beauty &
party snacks lined-up on a plate on the counter-top

not party snacks exactly, but there are straws
for moreish truffling — and a perfectly-formed ass

that points my way with a comely glance, I have
been fuelled into lesser-resistance, my jean-pockets

stay in the lobby — I gasp & gasp, then gasp — nip back
to the lobby for the safety in my jeans, returning to gasp

until each & every gasp is empty. Our pillow-less talk
has its own gulps & blows — apparently his ex came

with him for the test, said sorry for leaving
it six months — so he's been partying since yesterday

since the yes — since the *yes, but don't tell anyone.*
For over forty-eight hours I am numb, don't tell

anyone there, or anywhere else, and even then
it's just A&E, who take a test, and lose it, like I lose it,

like the feeling I am yet to lose, because there is nothing
to lose — yet — until the PEP doesn't work — and then

there is — everything — everything to lose and nothing
works — not blame — and neither regret.

Lone Wolf Sings Beethoven

Lorraine McArdle

The wolves gather at the edge
of the spruce and pine trees.

Mottled fur on their backs,
charcoal pewter copper,

rising and rippling in metallic tones
underneath the silver moon.

Moon rolls in the corner of the sky,
a giant spotlight, a roving eye.

The wolves do not howl, just a low
growl rumbles down the pack.

One wolf holds back, arches her spine,
sings Sonata in C-Sharp Minor and turns.

She has a different tune
to serenade the mooneye.

The forest trembles with pine needles
and sleeping creatures waiting for the sun to rise.

Aviary

Sinéad McClure

The Inebriates Reformatory for females, Wexford, 1911

Mary is a rose-coloured starling, comes from out the country,
damaged wing hangs loose, bone exposed like a half-sucked gigot chop.
I didn't know I was feathered too, until Mary told me.
She said I am a brambling, a brighter bird than her,
full of stygian porter when they found me
kicking my skinny legs, and chirping holy war.
The men, hawks swooping on songbirds,
the way they did up on Greatmeadow,
young lads cheering them on.

Nora, a snipe, her long beak full of sticklebacks,
Mary said she hit it too many times
and that we all have these crosses to bear.
But my man was a brambling too, bright and flighty,
never home enough to put up a fight. The starling
doesn't understand my lack of piety, changes me into a crow.
Underneath the hood of black and grey, I shimmer.

I refuse to be damaged, Bridie the stonechat agrees.
She says we have strong toes, keeps us perched in a storm
and each night she sings to me, her soft warble quelling tears.

Men fear us, if you laid all our bones out flat we could rebuild
each cell, roofless to the sky, watch ourselves fly.
Use what is left to beat them with, leave the shape of us
across their featherless bodies, our bird tattoos, indelible.

Miyazaki's Europe

David McLoghlin

Dirigible silence—'til an army mega-blimp surfaces
from a liquid cloud bank! We love the external corridor
at 20,000 feet, the crow's nest, sea of cloud in moonlight.
The tabby-faced woman and the talking fire, multiple portals.
Is this Italy or France? Littoral of sunlight and possibility:
always 1910 but steampunked. Delivery Witch *bildungsroman*:
start in a new city and rent a room, your cat finds a friend,
the woman downstairs is a baker and has one in the oven.
The thermals above the forest where you're attacked by crows,
the cove he hides his sea plane in. (Is this Greece now?) Beaches
only accessible by air or sea, we're loving the lap, lap: not a cat
but waves. You lived in the land of the ambiguous gods for a while
and worked in their kitchens, said "Dear No Face, no matter how
much you binge, it won't be enough." Your friend's an artist
and she lives outside town, of course the sensei will always live
outside town, with her talking raven. We love this, and want
to walk into patter of summer rain, hand-drawn, peace with notions
of 1980s saxophone in an Austro-Hungarian nowhere / always-land,
maybe Trieste, maybe it's Istria, Dalmatia, a hotel on an island
where sea planes park, pull up outside.

My Mother's Partner Calls Himself a Chef

Jenny Mitchell

Potatoes are peeled first – the size of my young fist –
skin falling in one curling strip. Then chop the spuds
in half, boil till partly soft, toss against the pan,
the outside mashed to make a crispy skin.

He stops to shake my shoulders, telling me to watch
as he throws spuds into a roasting pan. The oil is hot.
Prepare the meat – I look down at his hands – large,
thick, skin puckered with deep scars.

He's slapped my face many times, attacks
the joint, rubbing it with herbs. He slowly winds a belt
around his fist, breathing hard with every strike,
throws an object at my back when I run from the room.

The joint is put to roast. Boil macaroni, grate the cheese,
melt by stirring slowly. The kitchen smells of roasting
meat. I hold my breath. He curses, says I'll never be as good
a cook as him, aged nine but called a 'silly cow'.

Again, he makes me stand next to his arm. I step back
as he strains macaroni, steam splashing in the sink.
He pours the melted cheese, adds a tinned tomato,
knowing it will bleed, turning macaroni pink.

The gravy's made by stirring juices leaking from the joint.
We eat off trays in front of the tv. He calls me 'pig'
because I do not take a breath between each bite.
I push aside the pink tomato, stringy bits of blood.

THE RED DRESS

Jennifer Nevergole

no red is innocent.
—Annemarie Ní Churreáin

Steel doors
opened onto robin song,
morning recess

I was six
wearing my favorite dress,
ruffled sleeves, cinched waist

The monkey bars shined like a tiara
I ran for a place in line,
bouncing like a red balloon

My two hands slid
around the first rung
feet hovered,

Pushing out one catch at a time
legs rocked up and over, knees a fulcrum,
my dress a parachute

Face bursting like a sunbeam
my hair fanned out towards the ground,
fresh cut grass filled my nostrils

A whistle blew
sharp like a screeching car
followed by my name,

Stomach curdled,
I sputtered back to earth
Sit against the wall

My hands pressed the dress
to my shaking legs
I swallowed my tears like a lump of coal.

The Other House

Mary O'Donnell

All weekend, this house asked nothing
but that I was part of it, as much as
the umber stone of the sunroom wall,

the crimson kitchen and yellow teapot,
a gleaming chopping knife.
This house took me in hand.

Eat only when hungry.
Walk the salt air, see April pinks
and wild garlics along the cliff edge.

Follow the deep path to the water.
A rising tide spread mermaid's lace
in veils around my ankles.

I was held, touched by a whispering
underworld where grey seals dip and turn
between the Saltees and the Ciarachs.

Later, I made tea, broke off a hunk
of wheaten bread, spread salted butter,
then lay on pillows in the green bedroom,

which held me, touched my skin.
The moon outside lit the way
for all I knew,
    but could not see.

SOME BRIGHT FUTURE

Brian Obiri-Asare

creepy still and it's hotter
than a junkie's spoon.
a manic week
spent fretting in a mix of spice
and craving – the raw
and sudden pinch of home,
this salty hell
of a fugitive life, the tempting
pull of the road – and another night
turned to dark like a puzzle.
we're cruising
as a world of possibility
starts to wrap itself
around me. softly, as if
it won't let go. even as
I'm about to split off,
I know: scrubbed dishes
far behind me,
too much country strummed
into our kitchenhand
dreams, and then there's
the highlife
sitting above my head.
drizzled in sun
and perfect blue sky
and a wish for more
that throws open the flatness
of this country
made of splendour, the opposite
of splendour,
and a struggle strung out
over working visas.
and yes, even in
this delirium
I can smell the beat of drums.

and above my head, Venus
now floats
and right next to me
his face full of grace, Marcus
starts to palaver
with his Igbo swagger. so bouncy,
so free, before
I know it
we cross a border
and the moon swells up,
fills with promise,
too much promise
his eyes begin to water.
kilometre after straight kilometre,
this migration
better become
a wound to be healed –
a scar – never to be forgotten.
but for now
we're doing 130 and I guess
this is the country
we can't help but leave behind

White Nights and Mockingbird

Jane Satterfield

You're the queen of some claustrophobic
country, restless in a crown that reads
not every leaf is bliss.
                    Tangled branches rustle

with avian disputes. Soon,
the herald will arrive. In the chorus
of alarm calls, the vixen is vigilant,

nosing scent trails along the ground,
her fur-flash an illumination.
The wingbeats of small bats cruise

the air.
          It's late and getting later,
though a single card points to a pivot,
a way to break the spell—your cue

to banish signal flares and let
the ledgers fall away.
                    Go through
the rusted ornamental gate to rout

the mockingbirds—the many-tongued
who announce their presence
in whistles, scolds, and fluent mimicry.

What you hear as a forest of song
is a single bird
          stringing phrases in rotation.

Cork – Bean and Leaf Café

Colm Scully

4th May 2024

In a photograph across from me
I see the dustmen out,
one hundred years ago.
Brooms of mountain heather,
shovels for the horse dung.

Now, gum sticks remorselessly,
grime congeals in corners
between imported marble slabs.
Poorly grouted,
soapy in the rain.

They've stopped washing the streets.
Machines broke down during Covid.
Unable to get spare parts
they sit asleep in warehouses
off the Ring Road.

Their brushes soft and dry,
their chins down,
like groomed moustaches
on the gentlemen
of nineteen twenty four.

Tales of the Forest

Dechen Shaw

1. Artemis

The huntress shoots back with her eyes into the soft space
between his ribs, extracts the front of a blade still lodged
from when her arrow flew across a crowded forest.

She turns her gaze down towards mushrooms and moss,
damp and smelling of mould. Acorns dried
in the middle of the road are crushed: too much sun.

2. Dogs Gone Wild

Headlights swerve through the dark from a bus full of people
fleeing the enchanted forest. Shadows flash across the track
as dogs left behind scatter in search of carcasses to scratch
their tangled fur on. They are not afraid of bones
covered in rotting flesh. They are not afraid of flies that lay eggs
that grow to maggots. They know how to get rid of an itch.

3. Digging is Not a Destination

Merged with the otter there is nothing to find.
Together we watch over the waterfall
collapsing in on its own thrust, all that force
from the height of the hill – then slink
further into it.

4. The Secret of Ferns

The secret of ferns is that they know when I will die
by the way I fail to see them uncurl. They can sense
in my impatience to get inside as the plugs of their spirals
spread, invisible, and move the pressure of air – a spectral
green, a damp and immortal stand against speed.

5. Living Room Forest

Her lover gives her a tiger's eye bracelet, stringed round sockets looking out from her wrist. He tells her to practice grief in circles. When she stares long enough, they blink and she disappears.

Midsummer

Stephen Spratt

Bedroom 3

Night softened by the memory of day
smothers a room strip-lit by LED
embers. On the top bunk a host of teddies

offers the illusion of protection
as St John's Eve reaches its peaceful end.
The youngest girl sleeps silently at last,

freed by a prosaic dream from the fears
that crash into her mind like freight, fears
that the man and the woman tell her will pass.

Rome's longest day is born into darkness:
dragons blackening the sky, fire falling
from them like sulphuric rain on Venus.
All feel, but few see or hear the screams

that wake the man instantly, bringing him
to the bedside of the youngest girl, leading
him to soothe and coddle her burning skull,
tell her there are no monsters, that all is well.

Dining Room

The cat awaits his pouch like a crackhead
at a hatch, cursing the inability
of his suppliers to rise with the sun,

prowling the food area they force him to share,
still filled with a scent of sad dinners. Gross,
but no worse than the stench of the liquids

they drink at their distressed wood table
under the gaze of an art-deco bather
too graceful to have ever graced Brighton's

strung-out beach. The man was up late last night
again, bothering shelves full of pretension.
Visiting, once more, his little spinney of words,
the only frozen part of the vast forest

of verse he stumbles around in the dark,
circling endlessly, like a bloodhound
hunting itself. And here he finally comes,
thinks the cat, like something I might drag in.

Living Room

Light penetrates twice a day, piercing
a lattice of softly probabilistic
forms to ping a gilded mirror at dawn,

and returning deep in the afternoon
to slice through equilibrium with a smile.
An austere, slender faced Ghanaian

mask and its puckish little batik friend
mourn on a whitewashed wall, their hollow eyes
eating the sun. There is memory here,

and resentment. Perhaps even malice.
Lonely Planets and beaten-up foes of voodoo
economics stand on finely carved, freshly
asphyxiated shelves. Madame Butterfly

disintegrates in the forsaken Dead Sea
piano rolls, while the man's captured Laotian
hanging clings to the once good room's bitter
lime plaster. People stir behind a cold fire.

Office

Twilight. Reflexive air. Soft green lights
on a computer webcam blink themselves on.
Take in the scene. Talk to the other machines

capable of congress, and/or awake or waking
in a building that once housed nothing more
than sheet music for impossible lives,

but now seems like an archaeological find
of the far future, where analogue met
digital, imposter met syndrome.

Two office chairs roll in and out of shot.
A black pleather bed unfurls for the boy
and girl he hopes can patch the software
that led him, time and again, to constrict

his belovèd father's heart in a fist.
Evening serves cocktails of nerves and relief.
Outside, the scent of St John's Wort lingers,
selling dreams free of this savage gravity.

An Islander's Last Wish

Paul Sutherland

The last resident had to be forcefully
removed to the mainland, but her final
wish was to be returned to her island.

In the distance, a cliff's purpling tint,
the wind-met geo smoothed for the small
currach-like craft to bring her coffin ashore
to her first and final landfall. Her two sons,
in black, attend its arrival; a third in robes
stands ready to read the rites of departure.

In mourning, an island beach stays calm
with pebbles and boulders that bore-up
her craggy foot soles or youthful spring.

Her first passion and love was aroused
here, when her slip-of-a-body reposed
comfortable on this stony bed. She heard
the ocean leap in her night-opening ears
sensed history's close, the crushing of fears.

My Brother's Friends Draw Dicks

Molly Twomey

After the fire my brother shoulders the side door
where earlier he punched its swollen lock.

He jokes with his friends that his Xbox survived
as it's made from the same adamantium

as Wolverine's claws. Soot and foam swallow
his workout mat, his weight-lifting gloves.

He enters the room where he used to sit cross-legged
with a train set, a wrestling ring, figurines

of Edge and Randy Orton. He tugs at the burnt layers
of wallpaper to reveal a Peter Pan mural.

His memories are a skewer of marshmallows
held over a flame, a pack of Bensons

he was caught with and forced to smoke at once.
When he turns his back his friends draw penises

like thumbs-up on the rippled mirror, by the handle
of the bathroom door, between the skylight's ruptured veins.

This is how they cope with discomfort, dicks fat
as votive candles glimmering in every warped frame.

Extract from 'The Split'
Julijana Velichkovska

sometimes i'm closest to myself when i'm the furthest from home in those new spaces where i want to pierce myself and flow out to fill them feeling the new walls to press into every new edge to settle in every corner to merge with the new borders like a liquid that is poured from one vessel to another losing its old form and taking on a new shape a new form (of life) a new meaning i want to flow there fast as a thought to hit hard at the bottom and splash out up high then to go back down deep to go back to myself sticky and different with a new electron shell who am i what am i in this new space where the wind has brought me where i have fallen from the sky when all you see is all i am with no past no why you see a wrinkle and a scar and you don't know what made it or when you see water and you don't know it used to be fire you see a child and you don't know it used to be a woman you see a woman and you don't know she is a child you see life and you don't know how much death i carry within myself you see a hand over the water and you wholeheartedly offer yours i was hiding in the shade on taksim square *alone among people like a star among stars* in the crowd of strangers through the hustle and bustle and the noise suppressed by the masks only the trolley bell was free sounding along with the song of the young kurds *dervishi diyarbakir* and the cat was free too contemptuously posing for a photo in the bookstore that was her home the children who wanted ice cream not tricks were also free my footsteps were free and my thoughts far from g(orion) far from myself with some strange memories as if someone else's or from some previous life remembered

Plants at War

Stuart Watson

In the yard of our rental house
for the month of January grow
plants modeled after an artillery
shell exploding in the night,
tendrils of fire arcing across
the dark, like each of us do
with our puny painted pottery
and key-fob lanyards, creative
in the way the guy turning a huge
wrench on an even huger nut
in Lewis Hine's 1920 photograph
might claim authorial title
to our nation's industrial output.
Today we will visit the arboretum
to take in the extraterrestrial
weird and wondrous world
of vegetation living side-by-side
with us while we search the web
for something odd to watch.
Like silent sentinels in the yard
behind our house, a choir
of agave plants with spiky
attitude aim their call and response
at the all-giving sky, the god
inside our prayers, like the eight
satellite dishes decorating
and beseeching heaven from the roof
of a nearby apartment building,
downloading tequila flavors
for consumption during prime
time by exhausted day laborers
from the margarita channel,
their own lips rimmed with lime,
salted with sweat from hours rolling
sod for new bougie lawns destined
to die in xeriscape replacement
during the foretold imminent
end times war with California's sun.

What To Do
Partridge Boswell

1st Prize, Southword Subscribers' Flash Fiction Competition

If this is an emergency, hang up and dial Dolphin Rescue. Stop drop & roll then run out into the street, hands to the sky, waving your arms like a baboon in heat ululating in the key of high C. When the grid goes dark, drink a glass of juice while singing *My Bonnie Lies over the Ocean*. Blow a bubble around your heart. Do not pass go, do not collect yourself. Go directly to the panic room, lock your djinn inside and press play. Don't picnic. Go straight to the nearest Safeway and eye the produce. Let the cantaloupe handle this, do not I repeat do not attempt this at home with an Allen Ginsberg wrench. Go to the nearest invisible phone booth and remove your clothes. Triangulate your naked eye with Sirius & Betelgeuse, then send up a flare. Click your heels together three times. Home is where you want to be, not out bowling your floating head down the road.

If this is the genuine article, hang up and call the yawning abyss of your nearest ableist. Open the window but do not I repeat do not cheat. Deploy the fire ladder stowed in the kids' closet then sit in the closet and cry while fondling their toys and clothes. Forget everything you learned in home economics and run shoeless to the nearest animal shelter. Volunteer your eye for an eyetooth, your rod for a cone. If this is what I think it is, do not leave a message on this phone. Hang up and dial a licensed service dog who'll remind you to *Breathe* in a frequency you can hear and obey. If you're still fishing, for Huck's sake why? Oh & one more thing: Watch out for pieces of sky. They may be closer than they appear. To do this, you'll have to put down the phone and look up.

Among the Azaleas
Gary Finnegan

2nd Prize, Southword Subscribers' Flash Fiction Competition

When the lights go out, Malcolm knows he won't be sleeping in his own bed. He's deep in the bowels of the outdoor lighting section, comparing battery-powered lamps with solar lanterns. It's eight o'clock in the evening.

Doors arming.

The security system seals the garden centre's exits. In the distance, the echo of a metal bolt.

No more wandering staff, no slow-footed customers. No barbecue browsers nor water feature enthusiasts. Everything is silent and lonely and going to plan.

Malcolm began these weekday rambles around the vast aisles of The Orchard Lifestyle Hub after Kay's third and final heart attack last month. House plants, perennials, the patio furniture – it's never boring. Reminds him of Kay. It was her favourite place.

He takes off his jacket and fixes his favourite tie. Once he figures out how to make the fairy lights dance and the mirrorball spin, Malcolm pairs his phone with a Bluetooth speaker for their last dance. Then he gives himself to a hammock and sleeps with a peace he feared had gone up in smoke.

In the morning, a metal bolt slams, the security system beeps, a store manager flicks a row of light switches.

Malcolm waits until The Orchard has been open for ten minutes before strolling out the door with potted geraniums. Kay's ashes rest among the azaleas.

THE 1914 HARVEST IS OVER

Mary Shovelin

3rd Prize, Southword Subscribers' Flash Fiction Competition

The old man secured the corrugated barn door open with a bolt shot into the earth. Mice retreated to their bunkers, squealing. He would have to halt this invasion of vermin or they would decimate the sacks of oats stored there.

A sweet odour of dead grass rose from the bales of hay piled up against a wall. On the other side stood the harrows and plough, no longer shining as when used for the first time in the dew-drenched spring mornings, but now grubby and rusty, discarded.

The tractor stood in the middle of the barn, its red paint dull like congealed blood. Wax and dusters lay on the ground beside it, a task begun by his son before he joined up, but never completed. He had argued with him about this pointless job. Waxing and polishing something that had to pull trailers and ploughs through mud and rain! The folly of youth, wanting everything clean and shining. Old men knew well that what mattered was the result, the straight ploughing of drills in all kinds of weather. Tanks glistened. Canons shone. But they did not plant and sow, they did not reap and harvest.

That boy loved shiny things: the glow of polish on his boots, the sparkle in his eyes as he stood up to be counted.

As the old man turned to leave, light fell through a slit in the roof. A pool of dank water festered on the concrete floor beneath it and a dark shape floated in the middle. A dead mouse.

Overproof Jamaican Rum

Jenny Mitchell

My mother's great-grandfather
sold his son for land. The outside
child – meaning he was born of a raped slave,
not the English wife fuming at
the sun – worked for neighbouring whites
who carried whips into their fields. Sugarcane

made white gold rum, exported
to the Motherland, worshipped by the son
who drank until he fought the road, rising up
at home – a three-room shack – master
with a borrowed whip that scored
his sagging wife, knocked down

to be knocked up. Four sons reflected him
in a glass of rum, singing hymns up to the moon,
piss leaking down their legs. On Abolition Day,
they knelt to beg for work, fields still chained
to whites, though whips were buried deep.
These forebears stumbled through

high cane towards my mother, abstaining,
not to worship God. Her father knelt to rum,
digging up a whip, scored across her back
until she fumed at every man, nursed
a plan, sailing to the Motherland, whip hidden
in her uniform, spat on by the ones she served.

At home – a high-rise flat that nudged the sun,
beaming but the heat turned down – she whipped
her son. My brother hid his pain in welts, fell asleep
a final time. That night became his shroud.
The moon and stars went out when he was buried
near the land her great-grandfather owned.

2nd Prize, Southword Subscribers' Poetry Competition

After
Treasa Purcell

The wall is kissing the dashboard. I seem to have parked *in* the wall, which is odd as I don't live here. Pumping my right foot doesn't make a difference, the engine won't turn over.

Feck it, I can't be found here like this when the wall owners come home!

It's bright, then not. My edges have narrowed to treacle black. There's a rain jacket jammed in the steering wheel but it's white, not yellow like the one she was wearing two (million?) seconds ago. Now it's slinkied at my feet.

How did it get down there?

'You alright?' spirals a voice within a vortex—a blur in place of a face. I shouldn't trust someone without facial features. Besides, when I look again they're gone. My stomach flips at the stench souring the air, churning my Cornflakes breakfast and a wisp of a memory.

Have I woken like this before?

They'll want to see photos from different angles, with close-ups of the wall I guess. Sun flashes on a crumpled hood. The orange of a mangled traffic cone lifts the muted tone of beige paintwork. I zoom out. Sky fills its blue back in, fir trees unruffle their green. Sifting shrapnel from gravel, I shovel bits of plastic back into headlight sockets.

They'll be able to fix that right up, I bet.

I'm tired. It's getting dark out, or dark in?
Everything is treacle.

3rd Prize, Southword Subscribers' Poetry Competition

Fall Risk

Róisín Leggett Bohan

I didn't want to bother the nurses, my mother says
when we find her on the bathroom floor smiling

up at us, embarrassed that we'd seen her like this.
Her IV cannula rivering blood along the ravines

of her fingers that grappled to grip the frayed call
bell cord. She was lightning once — a quiet card

shark carrying home her winnings of crystal. Listener
of woes on the phone for hours, too polite to say

she was having dinner. She adopted every stray dog
I landed on the front door with. But she became unbalanced

after the virus, after pneumonia, after sepsis, after two falls,
after two strokes, after seven months in hospital

where my siblings and I etched the corners of her
death countless times. Now she is where we never wanted her

— the nursing home, where I fiddle with the bent aerial
of her transistor radio, trying to tune into Lyric FM, finally alighting

on Bach's sonata for cello. Then out of the blue, fuzzy and curious,
a drifting voice interrupts — a pilot hovering Cork airport.

My mother rises from her bed, says, *I wonder if they are taking off or landing?*

Southword Creative Non-Fiction Award

1st Prize:

€2,000

Publication in *Southword*

Up to 8 runners-up:

€400

Publication in *Southword*

We are looking for compelling writing, as memoir or as innovative essays or as an admixture of both. Simon Van Booy, Sandra Beasley, Thomas Lynch, Kim Addonizio & Yoko Tawada have all published creative non-fiction in *Southword*, why not join that illustrious company?

Limit of 4,000 words. There is an entry fee of €20.

.

Open: 1st April

Deadline: 30th June

Guidelines: www.munsterlit.ie

Seán Ó Faoláin International Short Story Competition

1st Prize:

€2,000

Publication in *Southword*

Featured reading at the Cork International Short Story Festival
(with four-night hotel stay and full board)

2nd Prize:

€500

Publication in *Southword*

Four runners-up will be published in *Southword* and receive €400 (publication fee).

The competition is open to original, unpublished and unbroadcast short stories in the English language of 3,000 words or fewer. The story can be on any subject, in any style, by a writer of any nationality, living anywhere in the world. Translated work is not in the scope of this competition. There is an entry fee of €19 per story.

Open: 1st May

Deadline: 31st July

Guidelines: www.munsterlit.ie

Fool for Poetry International Chapbook Competition

1st Prize: €1,000

2nd Prize: €500

Both receive chapbook publication and 25 complementary copies

Featured readings at the Cork International Poetry Festival
(with three-night hotel stay and full board)

This competition is open to new, emerging and established poets from any country. At least one of these winners will be the highest scoring manuscript entered by a debutant poet with no previously published solo collection (full-length or chapbook). Up to 25 other entrants will be publicly listed as "highly commended".

Manuscripts must be 16–24 pages in length, in the English language and the sole work of the entrant with no pastiches, translations or versions. The poems can be in verse or prose.

There is an entry fee of €25 for each manuscript. Entrants may enter more than one manuscript. The winners will be selected by a panel of renowned poets.

The winning chapbooks will be published by Southword Editions and launched at the Cork International Poetry Festival. They will be for sale internationally through our own website, Amazon and select independent booksellers.

Open: 1st June

Deadline: 31st August

Guidelines: www.munsterlit.ie

Southword Editor's Poetry Award

€1,000 for the best entry of three poems

One entry only per person

Each entrant for their €24 entry fee will receive a complementary one-year, postage-free subscription to *Southword*

Poems will be read and judged anonymously by Patrick Cotter, current poetry editor of *Southword*

The winning poet will have their three poems published in *Southword*

If you are already a subscriber, your subscription will be extended

Once a subscriber, there is the opportunity to enter, for free, other competitions which are for subscribers only

Open: 1st July

Deadline: 31st September

Guidelines: www.munsterlit.ie

Contributors

Kosoluchi Agboanike writes fiction, poetry, essays, and plays from Enugu, Nigeria. She is published in *Oh Reader, The Daily Tomorrow, African Writer,* and elsewhere. She is a 2025 Oxbelly Fellow.

Author of the 2024 Fool for Poetry Prize-winning chapbook *Levis Corner House* and Grolier Poetry Prize-winning collection *Some Far Country,* **Partridge Boswell** is co-founder of Bookstock Literary Festival and troubadours widely with the bard band Los Lorcas.

Dean Browne received the Geoffrey Dearmer Prize in 2021 and his pamphlet, *Kitchens at Night,* won the Poetry Business International Pamphlet Competition. His first collection *After Party* will be published by Picador in September.

Eithne Carson is an 18-year-old musical theatre student and writer currently based in Dublin. Her work has been published in *Paper Lanterns* and *Southword.*

Pratibha Castle's second book, *Miniskirts in The Waste Land,* was a PBS winter selection 2023. Widely published, finalist in Fool for Poetry 2024, she was shortlisted in Fish Poetry Competition 2025.

Eithne Cavanagh grew up in the idyllic surroundings of Co Wicklow, which continue to inform her poems. She has won many awards and has been widely published. Her latest collection *Wingspan* emerged in 2024.

Anne Connolly was previously shortlisted for the Gregory O'Donoghue award and the Strokestown International. Recent books are *Once upon a Quark* and *Feather,* Red Squirrel Press. She loves being a Great-Granny!

Polina Cosgrave is a bilingual writer based in Dublin. Her work appeared in numerous anthologies and magazines. Polina's second poetry collection *Cargo* was published by The Gallery Press in 2024.

John F. Deane, born Achill Island, is founder of Poetry Ireland and Poetry Ireland Review. His latest publication *Selected and New Poems,* Carcanet 2023; a new collection, *Jonah and Me,* is due from Carcanet in December.

Ajla Dizdarevi's work has been published in *The Hopkins Review; Plainsongs;* and others. She was shortlisted for the Bridport Poetry Prize and is the recipient of a David Hamilton Prize and a Fulbright grant.

Eamon Doggett is from Bettystown, Meath. His stories have been published in *The London Magazine, The Irish Times* and *Southword,* among others. He lives in Galway.

Gary Finnegan's fiction has appeared in *Flash Fiction Magazine, Howl, The Ogham Stone, Ropes,* and the *Irish Independent.* He has an MA in creative writing from Maynooth University.

John FitzGerald's latest book of poems is called *Long Distance,* published in 2024 by Gallery Books.

Nicola Geddes is a star gazer, cello teacher, soup maker, tarot reader, gardener, and poet. She is yet to decide what to be when she grows up.

Jake M.M. Griffin is a multidisciplinary artist from the Northside of Cork City. His writing has been published in *Southword, The Quarryman, Tower, Abyss, Flotsam,* and elsewhere. @jake_griffin_is_lost

Lucy Holme is a PhD student at UCC. She is the author of the chapbook *Temporary Stasis* and nonfiction collection *Blue Diagonals,* both from Broken Sleep Books. She won the Cúirt New Writing Prize for Poetry in 2024.

Rowe Irvin's work has appeared in *PROTOTYPE 5* and *The Stinging Fly*. Her debut novel, *Life Cycle of a Moth,* was published in June 2025 by Canongate Books.

Dillon Jaxx bio Dillon Jaxx is a queer, chronically ill writer. Growing up trilingual sparked a passion for language and wordplay. Dillon has won numerous awards and has been published online and in print.

Emilie Jelinek is published in *Poetry Ireland Review, Ambit, 14 magazine.* She won the 2024 *Mslexia* competition for *The Sky Around My Father* (Bloodaxe, 2025) following her debut, *Wing Formula* (Against the Grain, 2023).

Kasimma is an author from Igboland—obodo ndi dike.

Jack Kennedy is from County Kerry and lives in Dublin. He has been published in *The Storms* and *New Irish Writing*. Instagram: @jackkennedywriter

Emily Anna King (锡萍芳) completed her MA in Creative Writing at UCC and is currently teaching writing at an international high school in Massachusetts.

Róisín Leggett Bohan has work in *PIR, Banshee, The Stinging Fly, The Pomegranate London* and *Beginnings Over and Over* (Dedalus Press). Forthcoming poems in *The Manchester Review* and RTÉ Radio 1.

Kapu Lewis is a Welsh writer and poet, shortlisted for the 2025 Rhys Davies Prize, New Writers Poetry Award and published by époque Press, *Berlin Literary Review, Watertower,* and *MIROnline.*

Kurt Luchs (kurtluchs.com) won a 2022 Pushcart Prize and his poetry collections, *Falling in the Direction of Up* (2021) and *Death Row Row Row Your Boat* (2024) are published by Sagging Meniscus Press.

Aoife Lyall is the author of *Mother, Nature* and *The Day Before,* published by Bloodaxe Books in 2021 and 2024 respectively. She lives in the Scottish Highlands with her family.

Simon Maddrell appears in *Abridged, Gutter, Magma, Poetry Wales, SAND, The Moth, The Rialto, Unapologetic,* et al. Sixth pamphlet: *Patient L1* (Polari Press, 2025). Debut collection: Out-Spoken Press, Feb 2026.

Ray Malone is an Irish artist and writer living in Berlin, working on a series of projects exploring the lyric potential of minimal forms based on various musical and/or literary models.

Fidelma Massey has worked in bronze and ceramic for the over 30 years. She makes detailed, precise, graceful sculptures, using traditional techniques — clay and wax modelling, casting, mould-making (bronze) and hand building (ceramics).

Lorraine McArdle was awarded the 2022 Poetry Prize at Listowel Writer's Week, was a finalist in the Fool For Poetry Competition in 2023/2024 and Shortlisted in the Bridport Prize 2024.

Joanne McCarthy writes in Waterford in both English and Irish. She was selected for participation in *Céadlínte,* Poetry Ireland Introductions in 2024. Joanne is co-editor of *The Waxed Lemon.*

Sinéad McClure is a writer of drama and poetry. She was highly commended in the Patrick Kavanagh Award, 2024 and shortlisted for the Mairtín Crawford Award 2025.

David McLoghlin's *Crash Centre* (Salmon Poetry, 2024) was shortlisted for the 2025 Pigott Prize in association with Listowel Writers' Week. He teaches creative writing with a number of organisations.

Paul McMahon is from Belfast. His debut poetry chapbook, *Bourdon,* was published by Southword Editions. He was awarded the Keats-Shelley poetry prize by Carol Ann Duffy.

Clive McWilliam's poems have appeared in *The Forward Book of Poetry, PN Review* and *Poetry Review.* His pamphlet *Rose Mining* is published by Templar.

Zoë Meager is from Aotearoa New Zealand. In 2024 she received an honourable mention in the Zoetrope All-Story Short Fiction Competition and was a Sargeson Fellow.

Jenny Mitchell has three poetry collections and has won numerous competitions including the Gregory O'Donoghue Prize. She is the first Poet-in-the-Community for Cork City Council Libraries.

Elisabeth Murawski is the author of *Heiress, Zorba's Daughter,* and *Still Life with Timex. Alias Irene* will be published in August, 2025.

Jennifer Nevergole is an emerging poet and a somatic psychotherapist, living outside Philadelphia, Pennsylvania. She is currently working on her first chapbook.

Mary O'Donnell is a poet, short story writer and novelist. Her collection *tenderness* will be published by Wake Forest University Press (USA) in spring 2026.

Lani O'Hanlon's poetry collection *Landscape of the Body* is published by the Dedalus Press. Her writing is featured on RTÉ Radio and in various journals including, *Poetry, PIR* and *Mslexia.*

Brian Obiri-Asare is a writer whose work ranges across poetry, prose and dramatic forms. He currently lives in Sydney, Australia.

Jenny Pollak is an Australian artist and poet. Her first poetry collection, *Clarion,* was published in 2024 by Liquid Amber Press.

Treasa Purcell is a Kerry woman at heart, living in County Roscommon. Her work has appeared in *Epilepsy Ireland Magazine, Ragaire* and *Poetry Ireland Review.*

Jane Satterfield's newest poetry books are *The Badass Brontës* (a Diode Editions winner, 2023) and *Apocalypse Mix* (Autumn House Prize, 2017). She is a professor of writing at Loyola University Maryland.

Colm Scully is a Cork poet and poetryfilm maker. His poems have been published in *Poetry Ireland Review, Cyphers,* and *Crannóg*. His second collection is due from Wordsonthestreet in 2025.

Dechen Shaw lives in Scarborough, UK. Her poems have appeared in *IS&T* and *Acumen*. She is a Writing Poetry MA graduate from Newcastle University and also a playwright (Lucy Shaw).

Mary Shovelin is a Donegal-born writer living in Belgium. Her short stories have won the Bournemouth prize and the Write by the Sea competition, and have appeared in several anthologies.

Stephen Spratt is a researcher and writer based in Clonakilty, West Cork. His poems have appeared in *Poetry Ireland Review, Southword* and elsewhere.

Paul Sutherland is a British-Canadian writer-poet. *New and Selected* published by Valley Press, 2017. A *Morning Star* top ten book. He's founder of *Dream Catcher*. Recently *Child Roots* Partnership Publishing 2024.

Molly Twomey's *Raised Among Vultures* won the Southword Debut Poetry Collection Award. With Arts Council funding, her second collection, *Chic To Be Sad,* is forthcoming from The Gallery Press (2025).

Réré Ukponu has been published in *The Irish Times, The Stinging Fly* and *Internazionale Magazine.* She is currently studying Medicine at University College Cork, where she is a Quercus Creative and Performing Arts Scholar.

Julijana Velichkovska is a writer, editor, translator, and poetry festival organizer from Skopje, Macedonia.

Stuart Watson bio, honored for work at newspapers in Anchorage and Portland, has work in *Rattle*, the *Broadkill Review, Beach Reads*, the *Muleskinner Journal, MacQueen's Quinterly* and others. Links to published work at chiselchips.com.

Roger West. Poet, songwriter, singer, performer. A punk long before and long after it was fashionable. Scottish by origin, European by inclination. Writes and performs in English and in French.

How to Submit

Southword welcomes unsolicited submissions of original work in fiction and poetry during the following open submission periods:

POETRY

What to submit: Up to four poems in a single file
When to submit: 1st – 31st January
Payment: *Southword* will pay €50 per poem

FICTION

What to submit: One short story (no longer than 5,000 words)
When to submit: 1st – 28th February
Payment: *Southword* will pay €400 for a short story

Submissions will be accepted through our Submittable portal online.

Our Submittable account limit means that we can only receive 1,000 submissions per month, so if we reach this limit before the end of January (for poetry) or February (for fiction), the submission link will automatically close and we won't be able to accept any further submissions.

If your work has been selected from an unsolicited submission and published in *Southword* before, we ask that you please don't submit for one year before submitting again – for example, if you were accepted in the last open submission period (2025) it means you need to skip the one upcoming (2026) and wait for the next (2027).

Visit munsterlit.ie/southword or southword.submittable.com for further guidelines.

Printed in Dunstable, United Kingdom